Praise for Breakwater

"*Breakwater* is that rare ki[...]
mysterious and profound[...]
forth the unspoken paradoxes that lurk in every
household; the need to be sheltered versus the
desire to be free, the craving for intimacy versus
the inability to divulge one's secrets. And the secrets
Marijke Schermer writes about are big and dark and
violent. They show us that the wounds of sexual
aggression may be covered up, but never fully heal.
Breakwater is easily one of the best books to come
out of the Netherlands in a long time."
JOOST DE VRIES, author of *The Republic*

"This writer knows what she's doing, that much is clear.
Breakwater is a book that hurts. Supreme happiness
and its blunt violation are placed side by side with great
precision. Ineluctably, it advances toward a climax.
Now I want to read this writer's other work too."
De Groene Amsterdammer

"Her second novel starts in an exemplary and classical
fashion in all senses. Schermer work reminds one of Ian
McEwan's. But with the ending she then mocks the
classical form and norm. This is excellent literature."
NRC

"What Marijke Schermer does in *Breakwater* is incredible. The story—in language that streams and flows and
hits home—gets increasingly oppressive."
MARJON KOK

"Every time I read the first chapter I honestly think: this is so good, this is so wonderful. I like everything about it."
MARJA PRUIS

"An exemplary tale of lies and silence."
De Limburger

●

Praise for Love, If That's What It Is

"The author expertly humanizes each of the characters' desires and flaws as she illuminates the raw, inner workings of a broken marriage. This is as cathartic as it is gut-churning. ... A scintillating debut."
Publishers Weekly

"In *Love, If That's What It Is* Marijke Schermer dissects ordinary family life so subtly and yet so vibrantly, that it leaves you out of breath and makes you reevaluate your own most self-evident assumptions."
ROXANE VAN IPEREN, author of *The High Nest*

"Insightful and engrossing."
The Herald

"Marijke Schermer flawlessly analyzes how love takes its course."
Het Parool

"On every page Schermer excels with sentences that seem ordinary, but are packed with meaning. After every striking sentence, I had to put the book down for

a while. This book is about love—if that's what it is, of course—and who has not become love's victim?"
Trouw

"Schermer's technical ingenuity traps you, making you question your standards, assumptions, and blind spots. This is a big and definitive, but also investigative, story about love. Schermer is fast becoming one of the most interesting writers in the Netherlands."
NRC Handelsblad

"*Love, If That's What It Is* has the potential to become as successful as Herman Koch's *The Dinner*."
De Standaard

"Schermer's fresh style adds something really new to the mountain of stories about falling in love, unhappy marriages, cheating, and heartbreak—she seems to have cleared the dust off the whole theme."
De Volkskrant

"Schermer zooms in on the essential question of how autonomous you can still be when you live together. This novel has a careful and poetic style and is precise in its construction. Schermer effortlessly manages to infect you with the feelings of the novel's characters. *Love, If That's What It Is* paws and tugs at your fixed concepts."
Tzum

"Stories about love and relationships have often been told, but Schermer's approach to these themes puts it all into a new light and cannot be compared with that

of any other writer. Her work has been compared with Ian McEwan's, though, in which often a wrong step or decision radically alters a life for good."
Literair Nederland

BREAK
WATER

Marijke Schermer

BREAK
WATER

Translated from the Dutch
by Liz Waters

WORLD EDITIONS
New York, London, Amsterdam

Published in the USA in 2023 by World Editions LLC, New York
Published in the UK in 2023 by World Editions Ltd., London

World Editions
New York/London/Amsterdam

Noodweer © Marijke Schermer, 2016
English translation copyright © Liz Waters, 2023
Author portrait © Annaleen Louwes

Printed by Zwaan Lenoir, Netherlands
World Editions is committed to a sustainable future. Papers
used by World Editions meet the PEFC standards of certification.

British Library Cataloguing-in-Publication Data. A catalogue
record for this book is available on request from the British Library.

ISBN 978-1-912987-50-4

First published as *Noodweer* in the Netherlands in 2016
by Uitgeverij Van Oorschot, Amsterdam

This publication has been made possible with financial
support from the Dutch Foundation for Literature

N ederlands
letterenfonds
dutch foundation
for literature

Company: worldeditions.org
Facebook: @WorldEditionsInternationalPublishing
Instagram: @WorldEdBooks
TikTok: @worldeditions_tok
Twitter: @WorldEdBooks
YouTube: World Editions

Chapter 1

"ARE WE TAKING your car?"

"We're hopelessly late."

He comes out of the kitchen: tall, thin, a face that's markedly handsome. He's wearing an elegant suit. The saucepan in his hands and the tea towel over his shoulder testify to husbandly devotion. He puts the pan on the table and tosses the cloth back towards the draining board, narrowly missing. Leo lets out a high, ringing laugh. Alicia, the neighbour's daughter who's come to babysit, ties Osip's bib. In a matter of weeks she's changed from an androgynous child into a fairground attraction. Her cheeks and lips are plastered with red and she's wearing ridiculous, far too skimpy clothing. Emilia has to resist stroking the girl's head too. She kisses the children goodbye.

"You're driving. We'll make it."

She hurtles out of the driveway onto the road. The first part of the journey takes them along the dike, across the rolling river delta and onto a narrow two-lane road between poplars. There's a low summer sun with barely any strength left and a stiff wind. Sheep stand in the meadows to their right. A little later, on the highway, she can drive flat out, which she loves. They don't talk much. Into the car blows a memory of long trips south, singing, bare legs out of the window. Just short of Amsterdam they quarrel briefly about the best route to Leidseplein.

"You're probably right," she says, putting her own plan into effect. She gambles on finding a free spot, wins the gamble, and parks close to the theatre. They decide that paying takes exactly the time they don't have. They run and cross over, skimmed by a passing cyclist. Bruch calls out that next time they must take a hotel; for a moment they're seized by an urge to be swallowed up by the life of the city, instead of soon, no doubt again in a hurry, having to return to the silence.

They run into the Schouwburg, up the stairs to the auditorium, arriving last before the doors around it shut. He folds their coats together under his seat and pinches her in the ribs.

After the applause, as they're leaving the auditorium, they lose track of each other. Emilia searches for a while. Bruch isn't near one of the doors or waiting for her at the top of the stairs. She wanders the corridors. She looks at her phone. No messages. She decides Bruch must have found Vincent, director of the play and an old friend of his. She orders a glass of beer in the foyer. The actress playing Blanche redeemed the whole prissy production. She made every line of Tennessee Williams count, word for word. *You seemed to be gentle—a cleft in the rock of the world that I could hide in.* She summoned despair that erupted inside her like an unbreakable wave. Somewhere, through a chink in the evening, Emilia felt an emptiness she associates with profound meaning. It has made her melancholy.

She goes out onto the Ajax balcony. It's empty and desolate, making her wonder whether she's actually allowed to be there. Stacks of crates keep company with two parasols, blown at an angle. It's been raining. She searches her bag for cigarettes and finds none. She yawns. Then suddenly somebody grabs her from behind. A firm grip fastens on her shoulder. A big warm hand smelling vaguely of cumin envelops her face, pressing her eyes shut, fingers diagonally across her lips with fingertips on which her skin detects callus. Her back lodges against a solid body. Behind her eyes an explosion takes place. An immense flash of panic. Immediately after that, all strength and all shape go from her body and she slides, with no trace of a fight-or-flight reflex, utterly limp, out of his grasp and onto the hard rain-wet paving slabs.

"Hey, Emilia! What are you doing?" The delayed voice cuts through the thrumming silence. It's Frank, often enough a guest at their table. A buffoon, absolutely, and indeed in retrospect the possessor of that cumin-like bodily odour; she could have identified him by it.

"You're joking, right?" he shouts from above. At least twenty seconds pass, in which the damp of the concrete slabs soaks into the fabric of her clothes, in which she wonders whether a remark could undo her reaction. Only then does Emilia rediscover her muscles and bones and get up.

"I didn't mean to frighten you." He stammers on, saying it was only a joke, saying he wanted her to guess who he was, she knows that, doesn't she? His tufted black eyebrows give him a dishevelled look. He says he did it on impulse, and by the time it struck him as inappropriate it was already too late. She takes a cigarette from him, accepts a light, inhales. They smoke and look at the square below, at the nightlife crowd drifting between the trams. She shivers in her thin blouse.

"Must be scary as hell," she says, "to have impulses like that."

Again he says he regrets it.

If you say that one more time, Emilia thinks, I'll hit you.

In the mirror she sees how pale she is. She leans on the sink. A memory creeps up into her larynx of a summer's evening, a memory she'd successfully put into sleep mode and filed away in a corner of her system. The door behind her opens and they come chirping in, girls. She goes into a toilet cubicle and carefully shuts the door. Inside she drops her bag, gasps for air, strokes her throat. Then she puts her hands flat against the cold tiles of the wall. She's breathing again, but too shallow, too fast. She thinks she's about to vomit. She sits down. You're not going to die; it's breathing itself that's suffocating you. This is now. You're safe. On the other side of the door, the girls address the question of whether or not to go to a party. Their voices are clear and melodious. As she listens, she slowly gets her breathing under control, then slaps the blood back into her cheeks. She waits for the washroom to empty before leaving the toilet cubicle. She walks back along the semicircular corridor with its actor portraits, then down the softly carpeted staircase, passing Frank halfway, who is standing talking to someone, holding his tie with both hands like a lifeline. He winks at her, as if they share a secret. In the circular foyer below, somebody is playing records. Dance music, but no one is dancing. She orders another beer. Bruch comes to stand next to her and puts a hand on her naked back inside her blouse.

"You were here? All this time? I've been looking for you."

"Here I am, Bruch. Here's where I've been, all this time."

"Let's go, before anyone starts doing Brando." He hands over her coat. She drains her glass and they walk outside. It's raining again.

"There are two kinds of people," Bruch says under the portico. "People who can resist Marlon Brando when he yells up to Stella and people who can't." They turn the corner. He stops at the door to a bar. They've been inside before. She remembers he was wearing a green shirt. She remembers she'd had her hair cut that day and kept touching her head to feel how short it was. She remembers how clearly she could sense that she loved him, and how she drank a glass of wine before pulling the pregnancy test she'd urinated on shortly before out from under a napkin. And that Bruch cried. With emotion. She'd been on the point of telling him everything.

The bar has changed, although she couldn't say exactly how; it still has the wall with antlers and cuckoo clocks that she was looking at then. They order wine and sit down side by side on a sofa.

"What did you think of it?" she asks.

"I thought it was terrible. You?"

"It's such an amazingly beautiful play ..."

"Yes! Exactly!"

"I just love that play so very much."

"Yes, you already said that."

"Am I only allowed to say it once?"

"No, but once tells me enough."

"Yes."

"So it's unnecessary."

"Anyway, the first time I said it was beautiful. The second time I said I loved it."

"Minor distinction."

"Vital difference. I don't love everything that's beautiful."

"No, but you do think everything you love is beautiful."

"Do I?"

"Don't you?"

"I don't know. What is beautiful?" She hopes he doesn't say *you're beautiful*. He says nothing. She thinks of the game they used to play in bars. Dreaming up a life for everyone. Why did they stop doing that?

"Remember sitting here? It was here that we found out I was pregnant with Leo."

"That wasn't here."

"Yes it was here."

"No it wasn't. It wasn't here. It definitely wasn't here." He looks suspicious, as if she's craftily trying to smuggle this memory into the evening.

"Where was it then?"

"I don't know."

"So how do you know it wasn't here?"

"I just do. Simple as that. Hey, look, over there. Vincent. Vin!" Bruch sticks an arm in the air. Vincent walks over to them. He tosses his coat, his bags, and his bouquets of flowers onto a chair and plops down as if they've arranged to meet here and he's finally arrived. In his own inimitable way, as a variation on confidentiality, he leans forward.

"I've fled. Nothing to be done about it anyway. It is what it is. Can't change anything now. I know what I'm like. I'll go around explaining all the misunderstood moments to everyone. They'll tear me apart in the papers tomorrow in any case. I don't know why I keep doing it. First it's my idea, then it becomes my responsibility, and in the end it's my fault. Unless everybody thinks it's good, of course. Then they take all the credit. Actors. Untrustworthy lot. I don't know why I didn't just become a doctor or something respectable like that. Like you, Bruch. A doctor! Great! So valuable! Jesus! Which reminds me, talking of doctors, I'm going to do Chekhov, in The Hague. But guys! Hey! It's been ages! What did you think of it? Or no, never mind, don't say anything. Unless it's something nice. I'll have what they're drinking. Make it a bottle. I really got to the bottom of that play, believe me, I've got Blanche and Mitch and Stella and Stanley in here." He slams his fist hard against his chest. "In my heart. I am them. I understand them. In the end they all want to feel that they matter. In the end the search for love is what drives them. What drives all of us. Drives me.

Drives you, too." Emilia avoids looking at Bruch. Under the table he puts his hand on her leg.

"It was extraordinary, Vin. Truly extraordinary."

"Yes, wasn't it? Yes, it was extraordinary. I discovered things in that play that I honestly can't believe I didn't see before, things other people have always failed to bring out properly. Once you know, it's crystal clear. Once you know something, you can't comprehend how it could ever have escaped your attention. Emilia, darling. How are things with you? What did you think of it?" Bruch pinches her leg.

"Blanche was good."

"Christine, yes. Christine was good. She drove me round the bend. That woman only acts when there's an audience, in rehearsals she never does a thing, but tonight she gave it all she's got, that's true, tonight she was good. It's possible Christine is so good because she's in the same kind of thorny position as Blanche. Her husband's left her and she's on her own, and she's too old, just that bit too old, and she knows it. Cheers. Great to talk to you again. Finally people who say something valuable."

"Too old for what?"

"Too old for a beautiful new young love. Once she turns forty-five a woman needs to think three times before jettisoning what she has."

"But he jettisoned her, if I understand correctly?"

"Never mind, I'll spare you the whole story." He shuts his eyes and goes on in a tone intended to imply that he's jesting. "And I'm not in the mood for a debate about whether I've just said something insulting about women. Far as I'm concerned it's a neutral observation. I can't help it; saying something isn't what makes it true. The ending! What did you think of the ending?" He fills their glasses. They clink. Bruch comes up with a few charitable generalities about the ending, all of which Vincent interprets in his favour while drinking the wine at a furious rate. Emilia and Bruch eventually stand up and wait for Vincent to stop talking, which he doesn't. Emilia pays. Bruch interrupts him to say goodbye. At the door he calls after them that he'll come round soon when he has a day free, which he never has, dammit, because the bloody theatre always summons him back to the arena.

They walk to the car in silence. In a different mood Emilia would mimic Vincent. But it was too dispiriting, that monologue, the caricature he made of himself. Bruch sits at the wheel and starts the engine before she's even shut her door. He's drunk too much to be driving. In the silence of the car, along roads that grow increasingly deserted, she thinks about her confrontation with Frank. She wonders whether Bruch saw him. Wonders where he was when she was in the toilet. Wonders what he's thinking about. He takes the turning for their house and shuts off the engine. The road runs downhill, so they maintain their speed. Almost a minute goes by before they come to a halt. The silence sinks into the car.

"Vincent talked as if the whole rape scene was his own invention. A new insight or something," Bruch says.

"And actually it wasn't even a rape."

"What do you mean?"

"He staged it like something more or less pleasurable."

"Really?"

"To me that was the worst thing about it."

"I thought you said it was beautiful."

"I said I thought the play was beautiful."

"Oh."

"The play. By Williams."

"Yes, yes, I know who wrote it."

When she opens the front door, the kitchen door shuts with a tremendous bang. The boiler is roaring and all the lights are on. There's an opened bottle of single malt from the year of her birth next to the sink and the remains of ice cubes melting in their mould. The French windows are open and the curtain is blowing out like a sail. The tea towel that Bruch threw at the draining board earlier in the evening is still in the same place on the floor. Alicia is nowhere to be seen. Emilia calls her name. No answer.

This kitchen has been left abruptly and in haste. The air catches in her throat and panic breaks out as goose bumps on her skin. She drops her bag and coat on the kitchen floor and runs up the stairs. She flings open the door to Osip's room and in the shaft of light falling in she immediately sees he's in bed. She puts her hand to his head to check he's alive. He makes a slight sound. Warm, sleeping, whole, she concludes as she quietly closes his door and opens Leo's. The smooth white rectangle of his bed lights up in the darkness of the room. No blanket, no cuddly monkey, no Leo. She slams her fist against the switch, and the light makes the sight of the untidy empty room utterly ordinary for a moment: toys scattered across the floor; felt-tip pens with their tops next to them on the little table; clothes hanging out of the wooden wardrobe. On a stool lies a headless doll. For a second she instinctively looks for the head, without finding it. A collection of stones and shells and twigs is piled high on the windowsill. The curtain is open, the window ajar. She sees herself reflected in it, a smudge. She should shout, she thinks, as she walks soundlessly out of the room and sees Bruch coming up the stairs.

"What's going on? What are you doing?"

"Leo's gone," she says.

"What do you mean, gone? What are you talking about?" But she rushes past him on the stairs on her way back down. She goes to the kitchen, drops to her knees next to her coat and bag, and hunts for her phone. In a kidnapping every second counts, every hour a person is missing halves the chances of a good outcome. Why isn't Bruch running out of the door into the garden, why isn't he shouting, why doesn't he do something? She sees Leo before her, rolled into his duvet, carried off on somebody's shoulder. She sees him being hit, hurt, abused. She sees him being murdered in various ways. She sees his body in the river, in a hole in the ground, stuffed into bin bags. Through the open French windows, where the curtain is being hurled back and forth, leaves have blown in. She shakes everything out of her bag—tissues, tampons, sweets, pencils, a crust of bread, a USB stick, hair grips, notebooks, a newspaper, Playmobil figures, cash, loose membership cards, cigarettes, mascara, and a dummy.

Why do they live here? In the middle of fucking nowhere.

Chapter 2

THEY KEPT DISCOVERING new things: a third and fourth plum tree, a spiralling circle of stones once carefully selected by someone and laid out that way, gooseberry bushes, a heart carved into the trunk of the lime tree, roses, a dried-up well, a patch of mint and lemon balm which they christened the tea field. They found out that the hillock at the far end wasn't a hillock but an overgrown heap of rubble. If anything was ripe, they picked it. They made mirabelle jam. Cake mix combined with plums produced a gooey pink and crumbly sweet-and-sour pie. They made apple sauce and apple tart. A neighbour came round and pointed out the rampant ground elder everywhere. Bruch discovered online that as well as a plague it's an ingredient for soup or pesto. They were determined: they weren't going to tame nature; they'd turn things around and let nature tame them.

Autumn changed the entire look of the garden at a tempestuous rate. The prospect of further effects of the seasons, how momentous they'd be here, filled them with awe. They saw it would take ages to feel completely at home in this place. They took walks around their own land with Leo in the sling. Eighty metres from the house was a rickety jetty, the river flowing past from left to right, always left to right; like a line of poetry, Bruch said, on the evening they realized it.

At first they bought lifestyle magazines and visited kitchen showrooms. They made drawings and thought up variations. They wanted to knock out walls, move the staircase, line the attic. After a week they decided to leave the yellow 1950s Bruynzeel kitchen the way it was, and in the weeks that followed they abandoned their other plans too, one by one. The house, no matter how dated and run down, was perfect. For now her favourite place was the conservatory. The glass had a barely detectable discolouration that did something unbelievable with the daylight that shone in. She lay in the warm yellow dusty light with Leo on her belly and slept through the afternoons.

Bruch's new job at the regional hospital didn't begin until mid-October and Emilia was on maternity leave. They were together almost all the time. They unpacked boxes. They read, lay in the grass, gazed at the clouds, and swam in the river. They looked at Leo's calm and serious face. He was defenceless and at the same time apparently in touch with something beyond their reach, a connection that gave him autonomy. He was an easy baby. When he cried they could comfort him. He slept a lot and drank without difficulty. When pregnant, Emilia had felt disgusted by her bulging physicality, above all by the public nature of the transformation. But she no longer had any thoughts of that calibre about herself. She was there and she was not there.

One afternoon she gave Bruch a hand job while Leo was at the breast. She looked at Leo's little lips around her nipple and at Bruch's concentrated face. She found herself in a new universe, cut off from the outside world, intimate with a dizzying depth. There was no conflict between her body as her child's feeder and protector and her sexual relationship with her husband; it all flowed together seamlessly. Her happiness was a glow that made her existence vividly real and at the same time erased her completely. It was as intense as falling in love, but of far greater weight, so there was nothing fluttery about it. Not that she was without thoughts. It was more as if her personality had disappeared. She was a head and she was a body but there was no unifying shell, no responsibility, little reflection. She felt detached. Before she experienced it, and after it went away a short time later, the idea that this existed and was pleasant was unthinkable.

It occurred to them to give a party. Maternity visit and housewarming in one. It would round off this period without obligations and mark the start of the new reality. They sent invitations flecked with plum stains and shook autumn leaves into the envelopes. They tidied up and made beds for guests. They booked all three rooms at the guesthouse in the village. They bought chickens from the neighbours that were stunned, beheaded, gutted, plucked, and wrapped before their eyes. They hung paper lanterns in the garden.

"Shall we eat outside at a long table?" she suggested. "Or is it too cold?"

"It's far too cold."

"Jacob will think the place is a wreck."

"Jacob is a wreck himself."

"You think they'll all come?"

"Almost all."

"Shall we cancel?"

Leo started crying in the kitchen.

"Don't be ridiculous."

"I'm going shopping."

"Leo's crying."

She fetched her keys and purse from the sideboard and went out. She got into the car and ignored Bruch calling out to her from the doorway, throwing his hands in the air. She drove to the supermarket. She did some shopping. Then she had coffee in a café. She read the newspapers, glanced through some brochures that were lying on the table, studied the menu. By the time she finally set off home she felt sick. She took the backroads. Her blouse was wet with milk.

Bruch was angry. He'd been at a loss for three hours.

"He's sleeping, Bruch."

"For the past five minutes!"

"I'll wake him."

"From exhaustion! Don't!"

She pulled off her top and picked Leo up out of his cradle. He had to provide relief; she was bursting apart. She watched Bruch looking at them. At the red-faced child devouring his mother. At the equally red-faced mother with pale wet breasts sitting crying on the sofa. It was over: the hole in time, the vacuity of paradise, the idyll.

Around twenty-five people came. Friends of hers. Friends of Bruch's. Her colleagues Eddy and Martyn and Josepha. Mascha and Abdul, the only people they'd got to know together, on holiday in Spain, who'd turned out to live on the same street as they did back then. Both her brothers were there and Bruch's sister, Philippa, with her three daughters, who left after an hour. His parents looked old and stiff in their smart clothes. In the early twilight they showed everyone the garden, the view, the wide open space. They showed them the twilight itself.

"Look," Bruch said. "Look how the colour drains away, how everything simplifies into contrast. And soon, if there's no moon, you'll see nothing at all, not the hand in front of your face, guys, look!"

They got everyone to listen to the silence. The silence that hung in the garden between the rustling trees and the sloshing water and the scuffling of small animals. Bruch named the trees and plants. Arend, husband of the woman who'd noticed the ground elder, kept correcting him, until Bruch ended up saying of everything, "And this, ladies and gentlemen, this is the chestnut." He played the urban version of himself, the one that belonged with their urban friends, and who saw nature as an eccentricity.

Someone asked what it actually meant to live outside the dike. What were the chances of flooding? Her brother Jacob took the cigar out of his mouth and said, "Emilia and Bruch take pleasure in the risk. Living here stretches the family's statistical safety into a good fortune that's more precarious and therefore more meaningful. It could end at any moment. Uninsurable, too, so if things go wrong, which things always do, all that remains will be the very essence of existence." There was laughter, but when she caught Jacob's glance she saw the anger in his eyes. She ought to have stayed near him. He regarded her moving away as betrayal. She repressed a desire to disappear into the furthest corner of the house. She uncorked the champagne and sliced the pear tart. Leo, in a reed basket, covered with blankets, slept through it all.

When the spell was finally broken, those early weeks vanished into the domain of dreams. Emilia soon settled back into her old shape. And although she'd never felt as if she'd lost anything, it was abundantly clear that she had got something back, something familiar, something resolute.

Chapter 3

HIGH ABOVE HER is the ceiling. The cracks in the plasterwork branch like rivers. The sunlight falls in a pool on the parquet. She tries to guess what time it is. She's out by one hour. The vacuum in which you register the soft warmth of the bed before consciousness returns lasted no more than three seconds today. Then it all came back to her. The boys. Alicia. The play. Frank. Downstairs she can hear pattering feet and joyful voices. From far away the whine of a mower drifts in. Her throat dry, Emilia knocks back the cold tea she finds next to her bed. A hangover is the bodily equivalent of shame.

She stands up, pulls on a cardigan, avoids her mirror image and leaves the room. The kitchen is tidy, the contents of her bag deposited in a bowl. The whisky bottle is back on top of the cupboard. Although she has kept it for more than ten years and the whisky is now forty-two, like her, it wasn't particularly nice. Bruch gives her coffee and asks with a hint of mockery in his voice whether she's all right. She nods. But he's already turned away. Yes, she says, yes, I'm all right. He asks if it's okay if he goes swimming immediately. Of course, she says. She wants him to put his arms around her. He goes upstairs. Out of the corner of her eye she spots Osip sprinkling the floor with a watering can. Leo is lying on his tummy watching a film. Emilia grabs the newspaper from the table, takes the watering can from Osip, gives him a biscuit in its place, throws a towel onto the wet floor, and sits down next to Leo. After half an article the paper is on the ground, Osip is sitting in her lap, and Leo is giving a running commentary on the film. Bruch walks across the garden towards the gleaming silver water. He hangs his bathrobe on an old fence post. He dives. Into the water with his pale skin. Ploughing beneath the surface with his taut muscles. Why didn't she tell him about Frank? Because it was strange and embarrassing and hard to talk about. Because she's in the habit of not talking about things. During the first summer they spent together, when she decided not to tell him what had happened, she set the tone. I'm not defined by what happened to me, she told herself. On the contrary, it would slide in front of me and block his view of me. It's an act of autonomy to decide whether or not an event is allowed to play a role in your life. Is that true? Is that an opinion? Or was it merely an escape? Can she reconsider? Years after a question is asked, can you still give an answer? She remembers thoughts she'd forgotten about. When the man slammed his fist into her face she recalled the time when, as a child, she was given an injection in her leg. The doctor slapped her bottom; she was distracted, which made her relax and barely notice the needle penetrating her skin a few seconds later. Small as she was, she'd felt tricked by that transparent ploy.

Leo tells them the names of all the characters in

the film and Emilia has to guess whether they're goodies or baddies. That's easy, since you can clearly see from their appearance where on the ethical spectrum each is located. Leo leans against her and twists her hair around his hands. Osip attempts to balance on her raised knees and keeps toppling forwards, and each time he falls she tickles him until he squeals and tries to wriggle out of her grasp. Before she had children she didn't know that contact with them would be so physical, so sensuous, so limitless.

That fist stays in her thoughts. How many times did he punch her? Six times? Twenty times? Which punch was it that broke her jaw? Is it actually still possible to tell Bruch? Does she still know exactly what happened? Can you reconstruct an event twelve years later? That face she once thought she'd always know anywhere has gone from her memory. If she makes an effort to call it to mind it looks like Frank's face, but she knows for certain it wasn't like his at all, that the similarity is purely because of yesterday and is her memory's feeble way of telling her how little she can trust it.

"It's finished."

"Turn it off, then."

"I want to watch another film."

"No, Leo. Just turn it off."

"But I want to watch another film! That one was really short."

"Leo."

"Please, Mum? Mum! That one was really short."

"No."

"Will you read to me, then?"

"Soon."

Leo stamps angrily out to the kitchen.

Alicia had been blackmailed, she said. Leo wanted to sleep in the big bed, not in his own bed. She apologized. Blackmailed with what? Emilia had wanted to ask, but Alicia looked at her with such contempt. Bruch didn't show his face again at all. She'd sat amid the contents of her bag gasping for breath. Watched Alicia chalk her bank account number on the blackboard because she'd concluded Emilia wasn't going to get out her purse. Watched her calmly finish drinking from the glass she'd hidden behind her back at first, before gently setting it down in the sink.

Osip falls asleep in a corner of the sofa. She eats the egg that's waiting for her on the kitchen counter and peels an apple. Bruch has been gone for almost an hour now. Isn't that rather long, in a relatively cold river? His bathrobe has transformed the post into a red flag. Leo is sitting at his Lego. She puts a plate of apple slices on the floor next to him and lays a blanket over Osip. She goes into the garden. It's windy and even colder than she thought. She walks through the overgrown grass. Not long now and it'll be too tall for the mower and require the scythe. When she was a child, in the big garden behind her parents' house, she once laid a small square purple blanket in the shoulder-high nettles. Then she took off her trousers and top and sat reading in her underwear, concealed and captive at the same time. In the distance she could hear her mother calling.

She plucks at his bathrobe. On the jetty are his

flip-flops. The wind creates wide, sharp little waves on the grey water. The river is high. On the far bank two cows stand looking at her. Does he always swim for so long? Does he swim upstream first or downstream? She turns and walks back, vaguely uneasy and resisting the feeling. The house looks small, huddled in the middle of the garden. Under a big tarp at the side are building materials, timber beams, and a metal staircase. For the new kitchen and the attic conversion—at last they're going to do all of that.

Indoors everything is the same; her departure and return have passed unnoticed. Osip is asleep. Leo is playing, the apple untouched. Emilia stands motionless in the kitchen for a while. She needs to do something to throw off the feeling that's taken hold of her. She needs to get back into the daily routine and once again forget what she's resolved to forget.

She lets out an involuntary yelp when the doorbell breaks the silence. Who could that be? Sunday morning. Half past ten. Someone come to tell her Bruch has drowned? Leo looks at her. As Emilia puts her hand on the door to the hall, the French windows behind her slide open. She's startled again. She slowly turns round. Bruch is standing in the doorway with wet hair and a face splodgy from the cold. She stares at him. He uses the top of the doorframe to do a pull-up.

The doorbell rings again.

"Expecting someone?" Emilia asks.

"Sophie and Douwe, right? Or not? They're early." He looks at the clock.

"Shit. Forgot." Sophie is one of Bruch's colleagues.

She and her husband Douwe have promised to help demolish the shed at the bottom of the garden.

"You mustn't say shit," says Leo. "I'll let them in!"

"Okay. Tell them we're coming." And in a sudden upsurge of energy, Leo runs to the door while she and Bruch dash upstairs. He goes into the bathroom and turns on the shower. She goes to the bedroom. She's standing in front of the wardrobe when Bruch comes to stand behind her, takes hold of her waist, and kisses her neck. He puts a hand under her T-shirt, on her breast. His hand is cold and stiff from the river. She moans. "You're moaning," he whispers in her ear. Then he lets go of her. He disappears into the shower. She slowly gets dressed. In the bathroom she combs her hair and puts it up as the mirror mists over. She goes downstairs, taking a deep breath on the final step, as if diving underwater.

"How did you two meet?" As soon as she's asked it she longs to be asked in return, to hear their own story.

"We didn't."

"We never met."

"I can't remember a time when Sophie wasn't there."

"His sister played with my sister."

"We went to the same school."

"I was in the year below him."

"We had swimming lessons together."

"We played outside with all the children of the same age in the village."

"There were about twelve of us."

"His mother made clothes for my doll."

"We kissed for the first time when we were fifteen and sixteen, I think."

"Something like that."

"But by then we'd been going out for two years."

"When we went to university, I to Leiden, he to Delft, we were apart for nine months."

"It didn't work. We missed each other."

"We felt deficient."

"An excursion to make completely sure there was nothing else to search for."

"We'd already found everything." As if to illustrate what they were saying, she's been plucking grass from his trousers throughout this call-and-response, while he held out his hand to take the blades of grass and lay them on the table. As if even his legs are hers. Their hands are as coordinated as the left and right hands of one person. Was that exploration of a life without each other, a life with others, primarily sexual in nature or was it about something else as well? Is the intimate life of childhood sweethearts deeper and more intense, or the reverse, because there's no mystery to it, no unknown past, no gulf to be bridged? What is that mystery, actually? The fact that the other person has had a life that shaped them beyond your reach?

"And now we live next door to the house where Douwe grew up."

"In the street where you used to play kick the can?"

"Exactly."

"And your children?"

"Fourteen, fifteen, and seventeen."

"And they played kick the can in that same street."

"Well, it may not have been kick the can."

Bruch pours wine into their glasses and now he too is plucking blades of grass from his clothes. The development of a child into a man or woman of forty can't be without its detours and wrong turnings. Or can it? Is one precondition of lifelong love an open mind? Or a stable character? Or a lack of real interest?

"What about you?"

Now she and Bruch are about to perform their own bit of theatre. To tell a story that, like every couple's, has been dished out before and acquired its own habitual phrasing. The joint version of their story. A story that doesn't actually say anything. A story that hides the abyss from sight. She takes a sip of her wine. Sophie and Douwe and Bruch have been working outside all afternoon, while she stayed in the house and tried to devote herself to the children. She got into the bath with them, read a book in the attic while they played up there, and cooked to the sound of hysterical cartoon voices. She fought against sleepiness, against the languid tedium of the day. The other three look healthy and cheerful. They have work clothes on and dust in their hair. They have appetites. They've achieved something today, even if it only amounts to a heap of debris on a trailer.

"At a party at my brother's."

"But she doesn't remember that." Laughter. Always.

"Second time, so for me the first time, at the hospital. I brought in a neighbour who'd been run over.

He was working there. We met by chance in the hospital concourse. We got talking. We took a walk in the park during his lunch break."

"And you were?"

"Thirty."

"Thirty-four."

"We saw each other every day, but we didn't go to each other's homes. We walked around town, sat in bars and on café terraces."

"It was a hot summer."

"We lay in parks. Or took a tram to the terminus and walked back."

"We kissed on street corners and in bars and we walked and walked and talked about all kinds of things, nothing major." That was true. They told each other hardly anything about their lives. They were both over thirty, they'd collected half a lifetime of dust. But they existed entirely in the present moment, it must have been something like that, she can't remember any motive but there was a feeling of freedom and of living in the now: what they thought about things now; how they looked at things now. They were outside and didn't belong anywhere. They were the first humans. The summertime city was their paradise. They described to each other where they lived. He had a sixth-floor flat. A square thing, he said, with three rooms and a kitchen around a spacious hall. She wondered whether this whole circling courtship display actually meant he was in a relationship. If so, it didn't matter. There was only one destination their feelings were propelling them towards. If he was indeed still with someone else, then that would simply take a little time to resolve, and so a little time was all that stood between them and the destination.

He told her he used to live with someone. In the past, although he didn't say how long ago. She was called Mariette and she ran marathons. Emilia never found out more than that. She remembers looking at his hands, at those long slim fingers, and thinking of the patients he touched with them. She remembers him manoeuvring his hands under and inside her clothing and touching her, eager, firm, and precise. That last day of the beginning she asked him to shut his eyes and describe her, as accurately as possible. It was both terrifying and arousing. As if he was drawing her, as if her body moulded itself to his description and she slowly became who he said she was, filling the contours he gave her. She walked home feeling created anew. When she was standing at her door, tipsy from the wine and captivated by love, he came and stood next to her, her attacker. Emilia shared the front door to her one-room apartment on the second floor with six other people. Tenants came and went. She assumed he lived in one of the other rooms. It didn't occur to her for a moment that this strange man was there because of her. She said good evening. She let him in, she actually let him in; he didn't need to force any doors. He only needed to break down her barriers.

"Suddenly, from one day to the next, she no longer wanted to see me. We'd had a meal on a restaurant terrace. Lasagne. I was on night duty. Starting at ten. I needed to go in the other direction and she walked with me a little way, then we parted. In the morning I rang her but she didn't pick up the phone. I left a message on her answering machine. I went to bed and when I woke up I rang her again. Still no answer. I kept on ringing. I assumed I'd forgotten something, that she had other plans, with a friend, out of town, I hadn't a clue. I didn't even know where she lived. I knew which street but not which number; we'd never yet been to each other's homes, we'd only seen each other outdoors and in public places. That evening I had to work. I tried again that night. She'd surely be home then, I thought, but apparently not. I left another message. Worried, by that point. The next day I couldn't sleep. I rang the friend who'd taken me to her brother's party. Through him I got Jacob's number. He refused to give me her address. I waited till nightfall and rang her again and again. I couldn't leave any more messages. I went to work. A week later Jacob rang me. He told me Emilia didn't want to see me for the time being and I mustn't call her. She needed time to think, Jacob said.

"Wow. And how long did that go on?"

"Almost three months. I had nothing. Not even a photo. I forgot what she looked like. I thought I'd dreamed her."

Chapter 4

EMILIA WRAPS HER hands around her glass of tea and lays her head on the table. From that oblique angle she looks at him. He's emptying the kitchen cupboards, putting everything into boxes and crates. Down on one knee, he pulls out the saucepans. Clumps of dust swirl out with them. Between his shirt and his trousers is a white strip of back. From time to time he holds something up and she responds with a yes and sometimes a no. If no, it disappears into a bin bag. The success of a marriage lies in tolerance of each other's domesticity.

Bruch is a beautiful man. His proportionately large head with its coarse brown hair, those eyebrows, the soft mouth, the autonomous sparkling glance, his skin, his slightly dimpled chin, the symmetry of it, the combination of strength and softness, have a magnetic effect. Only if you see him from behind or one side and your eyes are not drawn to that face does it strike you how thin and lanky his body is. Undressed you notice his protruding hip bones and knees, and see that his pale back is speckled with birthmarks.

She got to know him when he was already complete, when he gave the impression of being complete. He was thirty-four. He had a white coat, a breast pocket with a row of pen tops sticking out of it. Internist, immunologist: interested in the ways in which the body turns against itself. He had a profession, he had a life, he had sideburns that were not adolescent or arrogant but perfectly in keeping with his face and his fairly neat haircut. He owned his own flat. She imagines having known him since he was ten, before he got that pronounced Adam's apple, when his body was still on its way to achieving its promised height. She imagines them having played on the street together as children.

"Incredible, isn't it?"

"What?"

"Douwe and Sophie?"

"Hmmm."

"Isn't it?"

He makes an indistinct sound under his breath.

"I find it incredible."

"All the same, it looks good."

"You think so?"

"Don't you?"

"It'd be just like playing mothers and fathers, wouldn't it?"

"Yes, maybe." He stands up and slides the full boxes towards the conservatory.

"What do you mean 'it looks good'?"

Bruch is now starting on the top cupboards, emptying them and piling everything onto the kitchen counter. Spread out like that, it seems far more than could ever fit inside the cupboards. Neatly arranged, things take up far less space.

"Bruch? What do you mean 'it looks good'?"

"Exactly what I say. They seem happy; they don't strike me as having got stuck somewhere. I need more boxes." He goes upstairs.

"I think it's childish."

He comes down the stairs, looks at her from the bottom step, stays there expressly for this purpose, his face full of disapproval, the beginnings of a reprimand in it. She repeats what she's already said as he puts the boxes down: "I think it's immature. I don't trust it. Why would you go on living with your infant-school friend, in your own village? It means you're not taking life seriously at all. Or at any rate that you're not the slightest bit interested in getting some experience for a change."

"Who's saying they don't experience anything? Maybe they experience more than we do. For that very reason. What is happiness?"

"Stagnation, you think?"

"So because you had a series of boyfriends before you met me, you've had experience, enjoyed life, picked things up along the way, reached adulthood ..." He has a look of undisguised ridicule. She thinks of the period when she smoked heroin with her brother. Recreationally. Something you'd never do if you married your friend from primary school. When she found out that he did it without her as well, that he was addicted, that she was merely the alibi, the shield at his chest, only then did she realize what an abyss they were edging around. She betrayed Jacob, called in her other brother, Viktor, and rang his doctor.

"... and they haven't?"

"Haven't what?"

"They haven't grown up because they got to know each other at the age of three?"

"Yes."

"Jesus, Em, who's being childish now?"

"It just seems weird. Cosy."

"Cosy is good, isn't it? In relationships."

"Seriously."

"I am being serious."

"You think they know each other better than we do?"

"Yes."

"But could it be that you don't see each other if you're on top of each other all the time?"

"Yes."

"If you haven't developed an outlook without the other person in it."

"Yes, yes." He sighs.

'Why are you convinced they know each other better than we do?"

"They know each other's family background, know each other's parents, whatever. They know each other's former position in the school playground."

"I know yours too."

Bruch looks at her.

"Seemingly indifferent, not really the boss, but still authoritative."

He laughs.

"Well?"

"If I say yes now, does that mean it's true?"

"Shall I show you the house where I grew up? Shall we drive to Groningen so that I can show you the view I grew up with?"

"Nice idea," he says.

"Nice?"

"Interesting. I'd like that."

"Do you think you'd get to know me better that way? Do you think it's possible to get to know each other better even after twelve years?"

"Yes, of course."

"Do you want to?"

"Yes. Why not?"

"I was an unhappy child."

"Yes, I know."

"Do you think it would help if I told you more specifically how I was unhappy?"

"Help what?"

"To get to know me better."

"Are we part of a project now, Emilia? The project in which I get to know you better?"

Regret is a killer, her father used to say. She hated him for saying that. He stood right in front of her bemoaning the past, ignoring her, any chance of contact or restitution drowning in that regret of his. But now she feels the same clammy disquiet creeping into her. She's already blown her chances. After twelve years their receptiveness to each other's secrets bears no resemblance to what it was in the beginning. In those early days every little thing Bruch mentioned sparked hours of daydreaming and speculation about the nature of his thoughts and feelings, the secrets of his character, the events of that eternity of thirty-four years of life before he met her. Every new thing he told her about himself turned everything else upside down; she rearranged the information, filling the gaps again to make a picture that always seemed more desirable than the previous version. You can't ever return to the way you get to know someone when you're first in love, that limitless interest in details and trivia.

"Maybe ..." he says, standing facing her and leaning forward with his fists on the table. "Maybe Douwe and Sophie had a similar conversation about us. Maybe they think it's obscene how old we were when we fell in love. Can't believe it's real."

"They think we settled for whatever we could get."

"Afraid of being left on the shelf."

"Maybe they don't believe I had to think about it for three months."

"Who does?" He looks right at her. The moment lasts an eternity. Then he finally straightens up and turns round.

"I'll finish this tomorrow."

"You do that," she says.

Chapter 5

WHILE STUDYING FOR her sociology degree, Emilia became fascinated by the idealism of nineteenth-century statisticians. She focused above all on Adolphe Quetelet, a Belgian who introduced statistics into the humanities. He was gripped by what he found. In his opinion, a collection of mathematical data provided knowledge that could be used to make the world a better place. He documented all sorts of things: the age at which people have the greatest tendency to become criminals, the months in which more people than average die, the relationship between living conditions and alcoholism, and so on. He coined the term *l'homme moyen*, the average person, and Emilia was enthralled by his ideas and his attempts to define the ideal environment for the average person to live in. She wrote her undergraduate thesis about him and became engrossed in the question of how quantifying the world could guide you to the right sort of interventions. She was also interested in how data nowadays help us to understand things, or indeed to conceal them. When do statistics truly quantify reality? Advocates of existing policy will commission data-gathering to support choices that have already been made. One study is ignored while another is blown out of proportion. So-called facts, long ago refuted by more recent studies, continue to turn up all over the place. An immense amount of research is carried out on behalf of parties with commercial interests. Even before she graduated, she and a group of friends, fellow students, set up the SOS, which stood for Systematic Organization of Statistics. They looked for the numbers behind news reports, then published statistical data and articles that presented an alternative view of the facts. In the main, they tried to put into context the supposed certainty derived from the numbers, by demonstrating that opting for a particular model or way of defining a group had an important effect. By explaining that the normal distribution is not a natural phenomenon but a construct.

They were hired by policymakers, lawyers, science editors, and product developers. They had their offices in a basement in central Amsterdam, where they read and wrote and calculated and interpreted. Martyn was the mathematical genius, Eddy the person to speak on their behalf or to make their findings public, while Josepha specialized in the food industry. Emilia had a nose for current affairs and initiated the company's publications.

They had decided to be selective rather than grow, but this issue kept coming back onto the agenda. They could hire people to deal with the research topics they were currently declining to take on while continuing to pursue their own interests themselves, an arrangement that would allow them to make far more money. The summer she met Bruch they were having fierce arguments about it. Josepha and Eddy were usually in favour, Martyn and Emilia usually weren't. Martyn because he was socially inhibited and completely uninterested in money. Emilia because she dreaded the transition from a group of friends playing detective to something serious, something with pension contributions and performance reviews. Also, she was secretly convinced that the life she was leading didn't really suit her and she preferred not to anchor it too firmly. Fantasies of escape continued to lurk. She imagined an anonymous life for herself in New York, Berlin, or if it came to that, Moscow. That summer, as she walked through the city with Bruch, she was investigating research posts abroad.

Mid-August, the day she saw Bruch for the last time, the day before the night she was attacked in her room, was the start of a short break. She wasn't expected back at work for the best part of a fortnight and she was thankful for that respite. After the first, worst week, Emilia gave her colleagues a watered-down version, telling them she'd been beaten up but other than that she was fine. When her paid holiday ran out, she stayed home for several weeks. Eddy brought work to her, always accompanied by a bottle of wine or something she couldn't possibly eat with a broken jaw.

Within ten weeks all her visible wounds had healed. She'd lost weight but felt it suited her. She put on a short blue dress and plaited a scarf into her hair. She walked, taking a route she'd taken with Bruch. The daylight was fierce and glorious, as if washing her clean, purifying her, helping to peel off the rind that had grown around her. She passed a bench she had sat on with him, a pedestrian crossing they'd waited at, a mural they'd looked at together. She slowed down only when she got to the park. It was drizzling slightly but the moisture gave a glimmer to all the different shades of green, and every now and then a patch of sunlight burst through the clouds, glistening in puddles on the winding path. It was magnificent. Perfect weather in which to reenter the world, she thought, before almost being hit by a cyclist who shouted "moron!" at her.

The OLVG Hospital stood waiting, unaltered, facing the park. She crossed the road, passed the smokers, some with IV stands, and went in.

As if Bruch was always wandering about here, on his way to his lunch break! That was the thought that struck her once she was inside, lost, amid the sick and the disabled and the pregnant, amid their visitors and the hospital staff, amid the cacophony and commotion of all those lives, all those ongoing lives, all those people. As if she could simply relive that earlier meeting! She followed the signs to a toilet and slipped inside. She'd been intending to say that she'd needed to think for a while, which unfortunately happened to coincide with a holiday and then she'd fallen ill, but it all struck her as thoroughly implausible now. The prospect of their reunion, and the firm conviction that she needed to heal before she could see him again, had kept her going. Had given her a goal. She'd been flung out of her life and was steadily working her way back in. The healing of her wounds had not been a period in itself but a non-period, a hiatus after which her life would resume. But how in heaven's name could she have imagined these weeks would be a gap in time for Bruch as well? She thought of his voice on the answering machine. How could she have been so stupid, through all those quiet weeks of doing almost nothing but sleeping and waiting, that she'd failed to consider this?

She fled, from her stupidity, from the naive idea that it would all be so easy. She strode through the park, fighting back tears, cursing. She got into the wrong tram, got out again and carried on walking. The sky had darkened into a flat ceiling, it was autumn, it was cold, the city and everybody she passed seemed hostile. At her door she looked around. Someone was walking towards her, so she didn't put her key in the lock but waited. It took forever. When she was finally inside she ran up the stairs to her room, opened the door, shut it behind her, and kicked off her shoes. She went to lie down in bed. He would have someone else by now; he wouldn't even recognize her. Maybe she'd embroidered it all, corrupted it, altered it, rewritten it. What exactly had in fact happened between them?

That evening she rang him. In the silence that fell after she spoke her name her courage slowly swelled.

"So, where did we get to?" she asked, as cheerfully as she could.

"To a deafening silence."

"No, no, just before that," she said.

He gave her his address and she cycled over. On the way she imagined how he would touch her. But she no longer knew whether she wanted him to. Nor whether she'd be able to bear it.

He was less tall than she remembered. He was wearing a dark-purple shirt, and between the tips of the collar she could see the skin of his chest. She wondered whether he'd put on the shirt after their telephone conversation.

"There you are."

"Yes."

He turned around. She slowly walked behind him into the flat that he'd described to her. She both recognized it and didn't. It was a spacious flat. Sleeker, more colourful too than she'd expected. He had a sofa. There were framed drawings on the walls. Would he accept the absence of an explanation? She stood ill at ease in the middle of his living room. She took off her shoes. He put on some piano music. She drew circles on the shiny floor with her stockinged foot. He poured her a glass of wine. She stood at the window, which was open a crack, letting in the autumn air, and looked at the street below. They barely knew each other. How often had they met up? Six or seven times? Why would she owe him an explanation at all? According to what unconditional rule?

"You've got some time off?"

"Three days," he answered. Silence.

"Plans?"

"Nothing special."

"Good prospect."

"You think so?"

"Could be. Yes. Pretty good. Or not?" Another silence.

"You look different," he said, without turning to face her. And then suddenly, as if stirred by that sentence, his gruffness turned to concern and he took her by the shoulders. "Is everything all right?" He looked so tenderly at her that she didn't dare breathe. She carefully put her glass down on the windowsill. She kissed him to escape his gaze. When she shut her eyes she saw the face of her attacker, his eyes full of hate and horror, seeming to insist it was she who was doing this to him, she who was causing *him* pain. While Bruch's tongue slowly circled hers, she saw the slavering mouth that had cursed her. As Bruch's hands ran downwards over her back she saw *his* fat hands, grey in her memory, crushing and thumping her. She wanted to dissolve into this point in time, wanted her memory of that night to be shattered in an explosion. And perhaps that was exactly what happened, but each piece of shrapnel pierced right through the present moment. While kissing Bruch she was standing in a blizzard of tiny sparkling shards of pain and mortal fear. She thought of Simone de Beauvoir, who described how the uncomplicated sexuality of a young girl changed during sex with a man into forced surrender, and she tried to drive that thought out of her head because it had nothing to do with this; not every embrace with a man was a kind of rape. This in itself would be her revenge for the violation: her reconquest. This was her chance. He must touch every injured inch of her body, she would give him access to every inch of her body, no caution—caution would allow her mind too much of a chance to connect all these acts forever with that and then.

She pulled her dress over her head, then took off the rest of her clothes. She felt the heat radiating from her; she felt him feeling the heat radiating from her. She slowly, methodically, unbuttoned the purple fabric that covered his torso. No hurry, there was no hurry, as long as her actions stayed ahead of her thoughts. That alone was important.

A sudden gust blew the window open. He closed it and fastened the catch. He took off his shoes, his trousers. If I can do this I can do anything, she thought, and she concentrated on every atom of energy in her body. She thought of his specialism, immunology. If I don't succeed in this, then I've lost, and my past will be an autoimmune disease that will destroy me. To her horror she thought of Dr. Phil and the idea that a raped woman is broken forever. She thought of the people in television programmes like that, who prove the validity of psychological clichés purely because they know them in advance and use them as guidelines. She thought of the bell curve, which looked like a safe shelter but meant imprisonment in the average.

He took her with him to his bedroom and she registered the scent of clean sheets and the sound of rain beating on the angled bedroom window. He was far thinner than she'd imagined. She laid herself down on top of him and tried to touch as much of his skin as she could with her own. She looked at his eyebrows and at his nostrils, at the way the hair grew around his face, at his mouth, how wide, how soft, how pink it was, at the skin of his throat, at his shoulder, and, when she pushed his arms up above his head, at the deep slope of his armpits with wet black hairs that stuck to his skin in perfect looped tufts. She lifted herself onto him and took him into her and then they both lay there, silent, and he didn't move and she didn't move and she felt the pounding of their blood and there were still shards of memory, sensations trying to gain ground, to conquer the inside of her body, that body she had never felt so consciously as when it was wounded. He pouted rather like a fish or a child and she saw a muscle pulsate in his cheek just under the cheek bone, and then they moved, first she and then the two of them together. In her thoughts she avoided every word that highlighted the banality of what they were doing, words that had once aroused her, and she thought: Everything is contaminated, everything except things in themselves. I can start afresh. It felt as if there were something that connected touch and intuition, like a new kind of sense, a detector of purity. That thought, which her slumbering self-censor found pompous, enfeebled her and she thought she was going to cry, but she dragged herself back, back into her nerve endings, back into her blood vessels. He floated above her. How come he's managing to attune himself to me so perfectly; how come he doesn't speak? She was once given a massage by a woman who said she should imagine she was a marine plant and her hands were the sea. The saying "your old self again" came into her head. But you'd do much better to be your new self. Bruch looked so young, like a boy; he was so real, more real than her thoughts, it struck her now. His shoulders shone and the rain was still beating against the window. She pushed his arms away so that his weight pressed down on her. He put his hands to the sides of her face.

Chapter 6

THERE ARE TWO of them. Their white van is in her parking spot when she gets back from taking the boys. They lug boxes of tools and a sawing bench inside. Then they sit at the table with drawings spread out but don't look at them. They silently drink their coffee. There's no need for much to be said. They know it all already. Emilia asks whether she needs to stay home. She doesn't think she'll be able to work with them in the house. They shake their heads. She asks where they're going to start. Upstairs, the older man says, the one with the puffy face. Always start at the top. He gives her a wink as he says it. It's starting to rain.

Since the move she's been working from home. Once a fortnight she goes to Amsterdam for consultation and spends a day or two at the office. There are nine people there now and they've moved to a building on the Singel. Eddy has become managing director. Martyn has left to work for an insurance company. All he does there is make complex risk assessments. It inspired Emilia and Eddy to include a teasing dedication to him in a book about risk reduction and the effects of security policy on safety. One of the things they discovered during their research for the book was the extreme variation in the security budgets of several large multinational companies, depending on the region of operations. In essence it came down to the fact that rational appraisals are made when such budgets are being decided: What are the chances that a given measure will save human lives? What is the cost of that measure? What is the value of that particular human life? In Africa the value of a human life is rated far lower than in Europe. The term "value of a statistical life," an ironic reference to Quetelet's *homme moyen* and the way businesses painstakingly hide their data, immediately spoke to the imagination and fired up their activist enthusiasm. They devoted several articles to it.

About eighteen months ago, one afternoon when they were the only people left in the office, prompted by Emilia telling him there was something very attractive about his social commitment, Eddy said, "Ultimately I'm nothing more than a mouth full of petrol in search of a flame." Then he kissed her.

"Yuck, petrol," she said with fake jocularity as she pushed him away. But he didn't laugh and instead put his hands on her breasts. There was nothing attractive about the look that came into his eyes then. Needy. Coercive. She thought of a girl who used to live next door to her, older by five years, who confided in her that men are at the mercy of nature, far more so than women, and that nature is a dangerous thing. She thought of the self-defence classes the girls had been given at her secondary school after a flasher was spotted near the cycle path at the back of the building. While the girls were learning how to deliver a kick, jab a finger into an eye, and free themselves from various holds, the boys played outside.

"Don't do that, Eddy."

"Because you're married."

"Not the point. Let go. I don't want you to."

He let go. "Not the point?"

"It's not because I'm married that I don't want you to do that."

"Oh no?"

"Oh no."

"Because it doesn't matter to you that you're married?"

"Because it's irrelevant to my asking you to let go of me. Will that do? Now stop it!" She pushed him away. He went to sit on his desk and looked as if he'd far from given up on the idea.

"Do you two have an open marriage?"

"Pardon me?"

"Does Bruch do it with other women? Nurses?"

"I wouldn't know."

"Doesn't it matter to you?" She didn't answer. She thought about it. She tried to imagine it. She couldn't imagine it. "Would you even ask him?"

"No."

"And you? Are you faithful?" He tilted his head to one side, half closed his eyes, stretched out an arm to her. He was waiting for her hand; he wanted to pull her towards him. The skin of his throat above his chequered shirt was red and rough. She waited until he lowered his hand again. Eddy was married to Yildiz, a woman who always wore stilettos and never went outside without lipstick. A woman who had brought structure and ambition to Eddy's life and who combined her own successful career as a lawyer with the genuine pleasure in presenting herself, if she was somewhere with Eddy, as the wife of the managing director. A person Emilia couldn't have a proper conversation with because every time she tried she had the feeling they were sticking to some kind of script.

"Do you have an open marriage, then?" she asked.

"No. Not at all. If I had an affair and she caught me, she'd kick me out." He looked extremely satisfied at the thought. The way he'd said "nurses" disgusted her suddenly. Why did he look so pleased with himself? It was a game. Yildiz played the fiery wife who would throw him out if he cheated on her and he played the man who was driven by his urges, incapable of ignoring an opportunity should it present itself.

"And if she had an affair?"

"Same story. And I'd beat the hell out of the guy."

In very many cases a marriage was nothing more than childish role-playing.

She powers along the narrow road. The sky is grey and heavy and the curtain of rain swept aside time and again by the windscreen wipers gives the landscape a monochrome look. It's too late now to be worth going to the sos. Perhaps she can ask for her police report from back then. Since that one time, she's never told anybody the details of what happened, so there's no account closer to the facts, no better test of her memory. The detectives at her bedside, the detail in which they got her to describe it all to them, the language in which they wrote it down, reflecting as accurately as possible what Emilia had said, but in a sentence structure that wasn't hers. One of the detectives read it all out to her for verification; she told Emilia's story in the first person singular, in a high-pitched voice with a Brabant accent. Emilia gave a brief nod and then buried herself under the thin hospital blanket. Everything hurt. Why did the man choose her? Had it been something about her? She thought of Bruch, who had described her that day, just before she went home. The look in his eyes. Emilia imagined him arriving at her bedside in his white coat, imagined that the very first time he got to know her body it was in its current state. A doctor who wasn't Bruch examined her with darting eyes and cool hands. He looked as if none of her injuries interested him very much, which she found reassuring. She fell asleep. In that week in hospital she kept dreaming about her childhood. When not sleeping she remembered, as an extension to her dreams, things she had forgotten. They were little things, neither highpoints nor low ebbs. It may have been a diversionary tactic by her mind, a way of forgetting the brutality inflicted on her, of bringing peace to her wounds, of giving her something to do.

An older man in uniform asks how he can help her.
    "Is it possible to get a copy of a police report?"
    "What's your name?"
    "Sorry, it's a general question, a theoretical case."
    "Theoretical?"

"Yes."

"How do you mean?"

"Would it in theory be possible for me to get hold of a copy of my report of a crime? Even if I didn't report it here and it's quite a while ago now." She has driven to the nearest police station, in the city where Bruch now works at the hospital, and where the cinema is that they sometimes go to.

"In theory a victim gets only one copy of his or her report."

"And if I've lost it?"

"Then it rather depends. The crime, the reason you want it, the amount of work involved for us."

"So it still exists? It hasn't been destroyed?"

"I wouldn't think so. How long ago was this report made? This theoretical report."

"Twelve years ago."

"Wait a moment, I'll have to ask." He disappears through a pair of swing doors. She did once receive a call, with the message that they were going to shelve the case because there was nothing further to go on, no progress in the investigation. The call took her completely by surprise. She was already living with Bruch and he was in the same room when she picked up the phone. She went out to the hall and stood there leaning against the wall, looking at the door. Something about a DNA database in which the case would still circulate, so if anyone was ever caught and there was a DNA match, then it would ... She'd wanted to ask what they'd actually done, how they'd investigated, whether she could get a summary of it all. How did it work? Why hadn't she heard anything sooner? Why had she never been asked another question? Were they giving up already? She imagined the detective seeing the phone call as something he had to get out of the way, his least favourite hour of the week. In front of him on his desk was a list of victims he needed to phone. Some became angry and he had to say he understood, which generally worked better than an explanation. She'd held back her questions, thanked him for calling, and hung up. Politeness and reserve are the best weapons in a situation where you feel abandoned. Emilia stares at the high laminated counter bearing the *Vigilant and Dedicated* logo, at the door through which the policeman has disappeared and above it the clock showing just after ten thirty, and she thinks of her mother, who had that particular act down to perfection. They shared none of the intimacy and intensity of the deathbed of a loved one that she's heard about from others. Her mother kept all her fear and all her sadness to herself.

"Less serious crimes have a tendency to go astray in the system and in theory they can be retrieved but it's a hassle. Murder and suchlike you can request from CID." And suchlike. "In theory everything is removed from the active system after ten years and archived, unless the investigation is still ongoing, of course."

As if you could report your own murder.

"Would I need to give a reason?"

"Yes, you would. And you'd also have to show ID."

"What might a valid reason be?"

"No idea. I'd advise you to try the real reason."

She thanks him. He seems disappointed that the

theoretical question hasn't turned into something concrete.

He's well over sixty. Perhaps this is his last day at work and the streamers are already hanging in the canteen to celebrate his retirement.

Someone comes in and the policeman shifts his professional smile towards a place behind her left shoulder. Emilia thanks him again and quickly leaves the building. She walks down the generic shopping street and goes into a shop to hide. In a cubicle she tries on clothes that look precisely like clothes she already has. She buys two pairs of trousers and an umbrella. At the bakery she buys a sausage roll that she eats on a plastic bench installed in a circle with other benches under a huge joyless slate-grey dish, which sits atop poles of various colours. This disc on poles was designed by someone, she thinks. On the bench next to her is a woman with a pram. She looks at the baby's face under its soft white woollen cap; it's no more than a few weeks old, still wrinkled, with none of the chubby rosiness that babies get later. Tears collect in the back of her throat. She tries to swallow them, blows her nose on a paper napkin greasy from the sausage roll. From the edges of the grey disc, water drips down, a commentary, churning before plunging into the overfed drains.

Chapter 7

OUTSIDE THE SCHOOL are several other mothers, holding up colourful umbrellas. They're talking about losing weight. About slow carbohydrates and brown fats, and how healthily we lived when we were still hunter-gatherers. How do they know that? Emilia's colleague Josepha has produced heaps of articles about dieting. Its rationality and measurability are utterly subservient to the enthusiasm of dieters and opportunities for the industry. She hears a reference to BMI, Body Mass Index, which used to be called the Quetelet Index, after her own Quetelet—an example of the way a statistical instrument can fall into the wrong hands over time. It was designed to measure populations, large groups of people that differed in weight and height. It became an indicator of fatness for the use of epidemiologists, then degenerated into ammunition for good intentions in the school playground.

"I still need to lose more than six kilos," exclaims the thinnest of the mothers in the tone of a punchline.

"Or grow another ten centimetres taller," she says. "That's the alternative, of course." They give her sympathetic looks. The units of the definition tell you enough: weight divided by height squared. That means the denominator is in square metres. No problem for the theoretical average person, but real people are three-dimensional.

She goes with Leo to eat an ice cream in the village. They sit on a bench under the awning in front of the snack bar. He's quiet, swinging his legs. She ought to ask him something. It's strange he's so quiet, but it's pleasant too, and she doesn't say anything. The cars driving past splash rainwater from the gutter onto the pavement, no more than half a metre from them. Leo looks at the toes of his shoes and licks at his Rocket. He's the child she least understands; he's timid by nature and demanding, and he has unhappy moods that make him turn inwards. Whereas Osip is generous with his good cheer, elementary in his reactions, and he moves through the world undaunted. And Osip has always fitted better into her arms than Leo. A difference that doesn't affect the depth of her love, but does affect the accessibility of the feeling. She strokes Leo's blond hair to rid herself of the thought.

"Is it nice, little man?"

He nods.

"What's the best thing you've done today?"

"Eating ice cream with you."

"At school I mean."

He shrugs.

"Well?"

"Nothing."

"And the stupidest?"

"Nothing too. Are we going home?"

"Yes. We're going home."

On the way home they collect Osip from the crèche. He storms towards her and wraps his arms round her neck. Their life expectancy is well above a hundred. And the value of that statistical life is more than two million euros. These little boys have another century left to live. If there isn't a war. If they don't become soldiers, perpetrators, or victims. If there are no ecological disasters, epidemics, or invasions from space. Even without disasters she gets a knot in her stomach when she considers that they still have all their growing up to do. She straps them into their seats in the back of the car. What did Bruch mean when he looked at her yesterday evening, leaning forward, fists on the table, saying nobody believed she'd had to think about it? So what does he think himself? It's strange that she hasn't said anything in all these years, but how strange is it actually that in all these years he's never asked?

When the boys are in bed, she decides to get some work done after all. Fulfilling your obligations is the least complicated way of escaping the madness. Bruch isn't there. Once a week he teaches in Maastricht and he usually leaves the day before.

Emilia edits a piece by a colleague about measurements of particulate matter. Over the whole country, especially the Randstad, lies an invisible blanket of particulates, breathed out by cars and breathed in by people, slowly killing them. But how slowly? That's not actually measured at all; instead it's determined with the help of models. The models rely on certain assumptions, which are themselves measurable and checkable. The piece is constructed like at least a hundred others she's worked on over the past decade and a feeling of intense boredom comes over her. She's lost all interest in statistics.

With that same stale reluctance, she reads the file *Clever*, about what difference the form and style of education make in drawing out the potential of clever children. Her main job is to write the report, but it's still at the stage of data-gathering; she needs to wait until one of the others has brought all the relevant studies together. Last of all she opens a document with the working title *The Target Group*. She doesn't have a client for it or anywhere to send it. Work like the particulate matter report and the numerical study of the effectiveness of one-on-one education for highly gifted children are commissioned by a few wealthy, self-important private individuals, and those create the financial space, and therefore the time, to write an essay like this one. At least, that's the argument Eddy comes up with whenever yet another discussion arises about what she should put her efforts into and what not. For Emilia the writing of this piece is a commentary on that discussion. Commercial clients always want to formulate their own target groups, so they can bombard them with advertising. Actually, everyone always wants to define groups. For Emilia the underlying question in all statistical research and so-called arithmetical truths is: What are you measuring and who are you measuring? Followed by: What does that mean? Ultimately division into groups amounts to taking a stance. If you decide to chart the ethnicity of criminal young people, you reveal quite a different starting point than you would if, for example, you divided them up according to social or economic class. The fact that doctors with a handbook under one arm can make a psychiatric diagnosis merely means they've categorized the symptoms, not necessarily that they understand anything about the causes of, or solutions to, depression.

Chapter 8

THE WATER SEEMS denser than usual, and there's something oily about it. She swims with long, slow strokes that cost her no effort. Like an aquatic animal, she makes the most of each thrust of her legs by floating weightless through the water for a long time after. She's been underwater for several minutes without breathing. At first she could feel plants moving past her legs, but not for quite a while now. She realizes she needs to inhale, and that she's no longer in the river, because she sometimes veers to the left or right without reaching the bank. It must be a lake, or a sea; where does the river come out, actually? How long has she been swimming and where did she get in? Not in the garden, she'd have remembered that. When she tries to swim to the surface she notices how deep she is. Or is she swimming down instead of up? She's lost all sense of direction. Her lungs are empty and she's starting to panic. How could she be so stupid as to forget that she needs to breathe? The plants are there again too, now. Long, strong tendrils coil around her legs, her waist, clinging tight. She tries to pull loose, suddenly doubting they're plants at all. They seem more like a hand, grabbing her leg. When she opens her mouth, something swims in, down her throat. She wheels her arms and kicks as powerfully as she can. She's choking. She opens her eyes. The sheet has wrapped itself around her. With waving arms she searches for Bruch but he isn't there. It's half past two. She concentrates on her breathing. Maybe she could call him. So everything can become normal and ordinary. But he'll be asleep and might get irritated if she wakes him. Why would she wake him anyhow? It was only a dream.

In Osip's room she watches him sleep. He's lying on his back with his arms up. Perfectly motionless, deathly still. She shuts his window. Then she goes to look in on Leo. His face is turned towards the wall and his body is hidden under the covers. She goes downstairs, takes the bottle of whisky from on top of the cupboard, pours a glass, and steps outside to sit behind the house, under the lean-to, the heavy rain like a grey curtain between her and the rest of the world. She lights a cigarette, then rings Jacob.

"What d'you want?"

"A chat."

"A chat?"

"Yes."

He was eight when she was born. Her father told her Jacob showed little interest in her as a baby, but almost all her memories of affection or comfort are of him. He used to read books about war strategy and medieval sects and the origins of life on earth. He knew that Jupiter is a gas giant. Physically, he was completely reckless. He would cycle with his eyes shut.

"Why aren't you asleep?"

"I was asleep. I woke up."

"Where's Bruch?"

"I dreamed I was drowning."

"In what?"

"Does that matter?"

"Maybe."

"I thought you didn't have any faith in interpreting dreams."

"As if it were a faith."

"Isn't it?"

"It's a way of thinking. There's always a chance it'll get you somewhere."

"I'm not interested in self-examination."

Jacob laughed. He was laughing at her. He didn't believe her. Or he thought she was making fun of herself.

"Bruch's in Maastricht. Do you ever refuse a patient?"

"Yes."

"On what grounds?"

"I'm a doctor. I'm there for people who're ill, people who're suffering."

"Jacob ..."

"Emmie."

"Nothing. Forget it. How's Viktor doing?" Viktor is the middle one of the three.

"He's in a relationship with a Russian. She's called Olga."

"Really? For how long?"

"A few months."

"Where did he meet her?"

"In a bar."

"Oh. And?"

"She's twenty-four."

"And stunning, naturally."

"Naturally."

"What does she do?"

"She studied nuclear physics."

"Okay. I take it back. And?"

"And nothing. Viktor looked pale, blotchy, thin as ever. It's completely incomprehensible how he does it."

"How's it going with Lieke?"

Jacob sighs.

"Why do you sigh when I ask that?"

"I didn't sigh."

"Yes you did."

"Didn't."

"As if you think it's a boring and aggravating question."

"I don't know. It's going fine. Lieke is Lieke."

"Do you not want to say anything about it, or do you not want to say anything to me about it? Is she asleep?"

"Yes, she's asleep. It's almost three o'clock."

"Bruch saw her. I missed it." Lieke is a judge and she took part in a talk show, in some kind of debate. Weeks ago now. Emilia is glad to have thought of it.

"She wasn't at all happy with it herself. She thought she came across as ugly and far too serious."

"Fortunately, beauty isn't an important factor in her work and seriousness is surely an asset."

"That's exactly what I said!"

"Whereas you should have said she looked gorgeous."

"Seems so."

"And you should have known that beauty is a factor for everyone."

"Yes."

They say nothing for a moment.

"Who was the last patient you turned down."

"A woman, well into her eighties. She had no memory at all of the first fifteen years of her life. Not a single image, not a single sensation had stuck with her. She was a happy woman, with a successful business empire and a big family. No troubles at all. She just didn't want to die without knowing what happened."

"Surely it would have been interesting to help her?"

"She was a very pleasant woman."

"With an intriguing problem."

"And there would be no guarantee that what she started to remember was true."

"So is there a guarantee that what you remember is true if you didn't forget it first?"

"No, none at all. Most of our childhood memories are stories from somewhere else. Photos. Constructs that add up to a history."

"But you can remember things."

"Of course."

"Things that resemble what someone else remembers about the same event."

When Viktor moved out, she went on living in their parental home for another three years. Her mother died after a long illness, and horribly. Her father stayed in his room and the few times she crept in to see what he was doing, he was asleep in a chair. He slept. And when he woke up he complained. He said that he'd thrown his life away. That he'd made irreparable mistakes. That he'd deceived her mother. That he hadn't loved them enough. He spoke in the past tense. He didn't give the impression he could see anything beyond a retrospective. He wanted her forgiveness, or her understanding, or perhaps he didn't even want that. There was nothing left now. That's what he told her. Regret is a killer. He said that too. She left and added her relationship with him to his endless list of failures. Viktor was the only one who still went home. He was immune to their father's lethargy, to the gloomy atmosphere of the house, to the emptiness of the open landscape. He did little jobs about the place and distracted the man. Bruch has never met her father. Becoming an adult was a liberation, leaving home was a liberation, breaking with her father was a liberation, never talking about him was a kind of freedom.

"And if the woman herself had found it a problem, if she'd been suffering?"

"That would have made a difference. She'd have needed to come up with a point of departure, though, if only an image. An image would be a start. The therapy wouldn't be aimed at finding the truth."

"But instead ..."

"At reducing the symptoms."

There was a silence.

"Why did you laugh when I said self-examination didn't interest me."

"Did I laugh?"

"Were you laughing at me? Or didn't you believe me?"

"I don't believe you. And I didn't laugh, by the way."

"Do you think intimacy and candour are synonymous?"

He thinks for a moment.

"No."

"What if Lieke never told you anything?"

"Never?"

"Not really. Nothing essential."

"I think I'd find that rather boring."

"Boring?"

"Yes."

"Oh."

"Emmie."

"I was drowning in the river at the back here."

"I'll come to you. On Saturday, or Friday."

"Is it that bad? You can't, anyhow. We're renovating."

"Then come here. What kind of renovation?"

"When we got here, when we'd only been living here a short time, Jacob, did I give the impression of being happy?"

"Maybe that was happiness. Yes. I didn't think so at the time, but now that you ask me ..."

Those first few weeks; those first intoxicated weeks. Then Bruch went back to work and she was alone with Leo. Leo was a quiet child. They moved in circles around him. She felt like an animal. She felt free like an animal that has only its nature and no responsibilities, no expectations, no ambitions, no regrets. When someone came round or when she went out to lunch with Bruch, when she went shopping, or chatted with someone in the village, she would play at being a person, an individual, she would take care to show that she hadn't been stripped of her intellectual faculties, of her interest in the big things in life and her worldly desires. That her child was an addition and had changed nothing essential. But when she was alone she was an animal. She would lie on the sofa in the conservatory with Leo and lick his face clean after he'd finished drinking. She would walk along the riverbank with his little body bound to her in a sling. She would growl at the cat.

"I'm coming to you. I thought it was terrible, that house: small, tumbledown, with a completely overgrown garden. I honestly thought none of it made any sense. I was convinced it was a mistake, that you belonged in the city, because otherwise … you'd get lonely. I was abandoning you to Bruch. That terrified me. I didn't trust him. I thought: Bruch is shutting you up in that ruin. You didn't answer the doorbell. I tried to look through the dusty, filthy windows, but I couldn't see anything. So I walked around the house. On the patio at the back was the basket with Leo in it. He was crying. I called you, but there was no response. Then I went in. Your house was a huge mess. I don't just mean that you hadn't finished redecorating. There was several days' worth of washing up in the sink and a pile of dirty laundry on the floor. I went upstairs. You were in bed. You were asleep. You'd put Leo outside and gone to sleep."

"Go on."

"I woke you up and you laughed so languidly and sweetly, like a child almost, like the child you once were. You stretched and said, would you go and fetch Leo, he's just outside the door. I thought it was despair, that you'd been driven mad by the crying and lack of sleep and couldn't cope with it all. But you seemed completely content, Leo too, and you both looked well rested. I helped you to tidy the kitchen and maybe it wasn't so bad after all, maybe it was just the washing up and the chaos, which I can't stand but which you've lived surrounded by for as long as I've known you."

"Bruch was away. A conference somewhere, abroad. I'd forgotten about that."

"And now? You remember now?"

"I remember, but is that my memory or my imagination?"

She lights a cigarette and pours a fresh glass of whisky, to which she adds water, with the phone between her shoulder and her chin and the cigarette in the corner of her mouth. She goes outside again and sits down at the spot where Leo's basket was in the story. Why did she put him outside?

"Are you smoking?"

"Yes. Is that allowed, Daddy?"

"I thought you'd stopped."

"I don't smoke. Not really. I only smoke occasionally. I can do that."

They both fall silent. A bat skims her hair. She wants to tell him about it but says nothing.

"I need to sleep."

"Bye, little one."

Chapter 9

SHE DRAGS HERSELF to the kitchen and attempts to stand up. Clinging to the sink, hands trembling, and barely capable of exerting any force, she tries to turn on the tap. She can't. There's something wrong with her fingers. She uses her leg to open a low cupboard door. She hooks her foot into a large pan and manoeuvres it until it's upside down against the sink unit, so that she can stand on it. She leans her upper body on the draining board. Half lying, taking care that the pan doesn't slide away, she folds her hand around the tap and manages to turn it on. She grabs a dirty coffee cup that's within reach and fills it with water. Her throat is so dry it's as if she's still choking. She can barely open her mouth, but she pours the water into it as best she can. It streams down her chin and what's left of her blouse. She realizes that her lower jaw is crooked. When she cautiously feels it, she discovers a swelling on the left side of her face. Her legs won't stop trembling and she can't walk. Carefully, as carefully as a trembling body will allow, she lowers herself back onto the floor, clutching the sink unit. Her chattering teeth cause intense pain in her jaw, so she focuses on trying to make them stop. She crawls across the floor to the small fridge. With her less painful hand she

pulls open the frozen flap of the freezer compartment. No ice, but there is frozen spinach. She rests
for a while with her back against the fridge and the
box of spinach held to the left side of her face. Then
she crawls the short distance back to her room. She
pulls a blanket out of the cupboard and lies down on
the floor next to the bed, panting from the effort all
this activity has cost her. Hours later she sits up. It's
daytime. The spinach has thawed and a greenish
liquid is leaking out of the carton. She inspects her
legs, which are covered in grazes and bruises and
trickles of blood, as are her belly and breasts. The
insides of her thighs have been flayed. Her throat
feels like one big bruise. She assumes her jaw must
be broken. She cautiously stands up. Her legs have
stopped trembling and she can walk. She stumbles
to the shower. Sitting down, she washes herself. The
water bites into her wounds. If she rings for an
ambulance, it might take her to the hospital where
Bruch works. She'd better take a taxi to a different
one. She drinks the shower water but it makes her
nauseous. She vomits and drinks again. She dries
herself and puts on sweatpants, a shirt, and a
jumper. In absolute silence she listens to the phone
ring and then to Bruch, who is speaking into her
answerphone.

"Emilia? You still asleep? I had a quiet night shift.
I was thinking about you. Will I see you this afternoon? Will you ring me?"

She calls the taxi company. She has no voice and,
startled, she hangs up. All that comes out of her
throat is a feeble grunt. Have her vocal cords been
destroyed? Is that possible? She rings again and

orders a taxi in a whisper. She wraps a scarf around her neck and puts on sunglasses. She fetches cash from her desk drawer. She goes down the stairs to the front door one step at a time. Her ribs, thighs, and pubis feel crushed.

She waits behind the front door until she hears a car horn. Beyond the ribbed glass, shoulders and a head appear. It's a struggle to open the door. The taxi driver doesn't look at her but turns straight back towards his car. That suits Emilia. She walks after him as steadily as she can. He waits in the driver's seat until she's got in. Her right hand isn't working. Perhaps that's broken too. She pulls the door shut. Not firmly enough, because the driver gets out, opens it, and slams it shut again. She gives him a bit of paper on which she's written *Lucas Andreas Hospital*. On the back seat of the car she falls asleep almost immediately. She wakes up on a moving bed, in a hospital corridor. Later she discovers that the taxi driver took the liberty of fishing the money, all the money, out of the pocket of her sweatpants. She is wheeled past the waiting room straight into a smaller room. The nurse helps her to remove the scarf and pulls off her shoes. Emilia can tell from the nurse's face that she must look terrible. Shortly after that, a doctor comes in. She asks questions then helps Emilia out of the rest of her clothes. Her wounds are cleaned, she's given an internal examination, and evidence is collected. She's told it's a pity she took a shower. She's given painkillers, antibiotics, and a morning-after pill. Several hours later she whispers answers to questions from a detective. Then she's given a pill to help her sleep.

The next day she has surgery on her jaw. People keep telling her to phone someone. A friend or relation who can look after her. She shakes her head and asks for a newspaper. She stays in hospital for a week. Then she's allowed to go home. The heat of summer has given way to autumnal rains. The nurse says to her twice at the door that she mustn't think it's her own fault. It hasn't ever occurred to her to think that. She buries her copy of the police report at the bottom of the kitchen bin.

Her bruises turn into patches of dirty yellowish green, and the tormented feeling gradually disappears from her body. The severe sore throat lasts another week, but then that goes too. She drinks tepid soup and yoghurt through fat straws, and water. She sleeps a lot and ignores the telephone. She thinks of Bruch. Of the evening when he described her. Of his hands. His mouth. She listens to his voice on her answering machine. Cheerful, then impatient, then peremptory, and eventually despairing. Jacob rings. Bruch has phoned him, too.

"What did he want?"

"To know if you were still alive."

"Really?"

"He asked for your address. When I refused to give it to him, he asked when I last saw you or spoke to you."

"And what did you say?"

"That it was none of his fucking business."

"Uh-huh."

"He asked whether I was sure you weren't dead. He made me promise to go and check everything was all right with you."

"And?"

"That's for you to say."

"No, I mean, what did you tell him?"

"I asked him why he thought you were dead. He said you hadn't rung him back. I asked whether it had ever occurred to him that you might simply not feel like talking to him—an idea from which he derived the impossibility of any such explanation. Which I thought unbelievable. What a character!" Jacob's voice is saturated with disapproval.

"And?"

"What?"

"What did he say?"

"You sound odd. Your voice sounds odd."

"I've got a throat infection."

"Oh, really?"

"Really."

"He said he wasn't stupid, that the way you parted the last time didn't exactly justify the conclusion that you were now unreachable and refusing to explain why."

"Hm."

"You've got something going with the guy?"

"Maybe."

"Possessive type."

"No, he isn't. Or I don't think he is."

"He rings me because he can't reach you! I don't even know him."

"True."

"You don't think that's possessive?"

"There's been a long silence ..."

"Yes. But not endless. Because at any rate you're not dead."

"Just tell him everything's fine, that I need time to think, and it might take a few weeks."

"Or do I know him?" Jacob asked.

"He was at your birthday party."

"Is he that doctor?"

"What doctor?"

"That thin one. Friend of Jan's. Sunday watercolourist type. Bit of a ninny. That one?"

"Jake, I'm tired. I'm going to hang up."

"Shall I come and look after you?"

"No. Thank you."

"Is something wrong?"

"It's over already. I want to be alone."

"Okay, Emmie. Whatever you want."

"Don't give him my address."

"Of course not. Em?"

"Yes."

"You do know that I'm fairly good at looking after sick people?"

"Are you?"

"I heat soup, I read aloud, I like providing drinks for sore throats." And after half a minute's silence, "You still there?"

"No ..."

"I'm coming round."

"I'm going to sleep."

"I'm coming round. There's something wrong."

"If you come round I won't let you in."

"If you don't let me in I'll kick the door down. You still there?"

"No."

"What will you do if I kick the door down?"

"Jake. Stop. I'm not in the mood. Okay? Stop."

"In Scotland they said to me, look for something to care for, a dog, or a plant."

"I'm hanging up."

"Emil?"

"No."

"Sleep well."

She does her shopping late at the 24/7. She reads and watches TV. She spends hours looking at the street below her window. Tourists. Groups of teenagers. Children clinging to their parents' hands. Parents clinging to their children's hands. Couples. Hand in hand. Unable to stop touching each other. Hand in hand but still miserable. She pretends to be an extraterrestrial studying people from her space shuttle. One time she thinks she can see Bruch on his bicycle. She represses a desire to ring Jacob and ask whether he's passed on her message. She'd rather he didn't know how important it is to her. If she wants to leave open the possibility of seeing Bruch again, the chance of carrying on where they left off, then she must wait patiently and withdraw into the shadows. If Bruch were to know what has happened to her, he'd be worried. He'd be frightened of touching her. He'd want to spare her. He'd be careful. He'd treat her like a victim. He wouldn't dare let himself go. Or he'd leave, removing himself from her as far as possible, as quickly as possible. That's what she thinks as she sits with her feet on the windowsill, slurping her porridge.

Chapter 10

SHE HASN'T SLEPT for more than a couple of hours when Osip strokes her awake with his podgy little hands.

"I'm here."

"I see you."

He snuggles up against her and sings into her hair. She wants to sleep. It's half past six. "Mummy, Mummy, Mummy," he sings in her ear. He climbs up to lie on top of her and pushes her face into strange folds. Ought she to ask Bruch about his memories of those first weeks here? Or not? If memories are so unreliable, what could his version do other than contaminate her own without telling her what was true? The whisky has to go. And she needs to get up, to be ready in time for those men in their overalls, the young lad who says nothing and the older one who gives her dirty looks. She knows what he's thinking. Perhaps she could leave till they've finished here. Perhaps she could go with the boys to stay with Jacob in Amsterdam until it's all done. She could hire a babysitter; that would surely be possible. Maybe Josepha knows someone. She could work in the office and go out at night. See people. Escape this churning torrent of thoughts, this rut she's landed in where she continually thinks about the rape and about Bruch in the beginning. About time, which is irreversible and can never transport her back to earlier years, can never give her a chance to do things differently: not go home that night, not let her attacker in. Or at any rate ring someone immediately afterwards. Tell Bruch about it. Go and seek out her father and reconcile with him before he loses his powers of comprehension. She can never be young again. Is it true, what Jacob thought: Has she grown lonely? Was it stupid to rely so completely on Bruch? Was it a mistake to retreat to the isolation that a family is, which becomes even more isolated if it withdraws holus-bolus to a house like this? Now they're building an expensive luxury kitchen, and they're dividing the attic up into separate rooms. They've demolished the shed. You couldn't call this an experiment any longer. Bruch would find it ridiculous if she said that out loud. For him it was never an experiment. Bruch loves nature, exercise, cold early mornings. Bruch would have been better off with a different kind of wife, a stable, sports-loving woman like Sophie. While she expressed her horror, he hid his envy. Was that true? Does she know him? She knows what she's hiding but not what he's hiding.

"Mummy!!"

"Shhh!"

"Get up."

"Ow, not so loud. Yes. We're getting up."

"Mummy."

"Yes."

"Mummy."

"Yes!"

"I'm a princess."

They go downstairs, Osip with a shawl draped around him, she in her nightshirt. She makes coffee and tea, throws open the French windows, and hides the ashtray on the lowest part of the roof. Leo starts yelling Mummy-Mummy-Mummy from upstairs. She ignores it for a while then goes up to him. He's standing on his bed, red-faced and shouting.

"Yes!" She goes over to him and grabs him by the arms. "Jesus! Leo, I'm not deaf!"

"Why didn't you come then?"

"I was busy."

"But I was calling you."

"I'm not your slave." That's what her mother used to say. She wants to drive the sentence out of the room. "What's the matter?" She opens the window. It's raining. Again, or still.

"I've lost my flint."

"What d'you mean, lost? What flint?"

"My flint."

"What does it look like?"

"Like a flint."

"Okay, Leo, why don't you go and make coffee and sandwiches and get the schoolbags ready and get Osip dressed, and I'll look for a flint that doesn't have a description in all this mess."

Leo starts crying.

"Stop crying!"

"I'm allowed to be unhappy, aren't I?" Leo is shouting too.

She sits on the bed and for a full minute doesn't say or do anything. Then she picks him up and puts him in her lap. A stiff, defiant body. She strokes him until he stops crying.

"Sorry, Mummy."

"That's all right sweetie."

They go downstairs and again she thinks about those rooms in the attic, the new kitchen, the futureproofing it will give their house and with it their life. She makes sandwiches. Then she sits down. Motionless at the kitchen table, ignoring the chatter and squabbling of her sons, she clutches her coffee cup.

After she's taken them to school and the crèche, and spent some time sitting in her car scrutinizing the cheerful ordinariness of other mothers and the occasional father—she can no longer spot the BMI types, with those raincoats they all merge into one another even more than usual—she rings Bruch and says on his voicemail that she can't stand those men (Neanderthals she calls them) and he must ring her. She's conscious of her blunt, unreasonable tone. While she's scrolling to Jacob's number there's a tap on her side window. It startles her. She's become ridiculously jittery, dammit. The smiling face of what's-her-name-again under an umbrella. She winds the window down.

"Hey, Emilia, we were wondering if you felt like coming for a cup of coffee." Bright blue eyes in a too-round, too-blonde, too-soft, too-untroubled face. Beyond her she sees the mother of Sam and the mother of Maya and the mother of what's-his-name-again. She smiles at them. "We do it every Wednesday." They smile back. She declines the invitation, grins broadly at everybody one more time, then winds up her window. Jacob doesn't answer her call. She rings Josepha to ask whether she knows of a babysitter for a week.

"Emilia, can I interrupt you for a moment? You haven't looked at your mails yet, I take it?"

"No."

"Marieke has accused Eddy of sexual assault and intimidation."

Marieke is Eddy's intern, early twenties, bright, attractive, slightly shy.

"She's reported him, as well."

Emilia knows immediately that it's true. "And Eddy?"

"Denies it."

Of course.

"I support him," Josepha says.

"What?"

"He wouldn't lie to me. Not to me."

"It's true. I know it is. I know Eddy too. We're old enough to say no, but ... Jos, you know it as well as I do. It's true."

"Or to say yes."

"What? Yes. Or to say yes." Is she talking about herself?

The river has doubled in size after all the rain. The meadows are empty; all the sheep have gone. Desolate willows stand up to their trunks in the water, at its mercy. She turns the ventilator to its highest setting to drive the moisture off the windscreen. With Leo and Osip safely stowed at school and the crèche, she loves them more than at any other time. From this distance she can feel the love instead of drowning in it. Will her own parents have experienced that, thought about it, about that mixture of love and imprisonment, the chronic fatigue caused not just by lack of sleep but by an overloaded brain, by continually having to know where they are, see what they need, estimate which dangers around them must be eliminated? Her parents never gave the impression that having children had interfered with their lives, that life had ever been any different. They did sometimes tell her a bit about their own childhoods, but never about the period between being a child and being a parent, their free adult lives. Didn't they ever have such a thing? Or wasn't she interested in hearing about it?

Bruch rings. He's listened to her voicemail, she assumes, but he doesn't say anything about it. She tells him about Eddy. The subject slips into the place of her misery. All you need is for things to keep happening, external things that can distract you.

"I don't like him." Every time she talks about Eddy for more than a minute, or after Bruch has seen him, he says that.

"I know. Where are you?"

"I'm in the atrium at the university."

"With your bag at your feet and your jacket over one leg?"

"Yes." He chuckles.

"What do you think, if you look at yourself from a distance? Do you look professorial? Or more like a slightly older student?"

"Discuss. Perhaps still mainly like a doctor gone astray."

"Sorry about that voicemail."

"Drive carefully."

She turns onto the highway and accelerates. Driving always has a calming effect on her.

She parks on the north bank of the IJ and takes the ferry. Once she's past the bustle of Amsterdam Central Station she turns right, left, right, and into Spuistraat. She hears someone call her name from the far side of the street. It's Vincent. She sticks up a hand and wants to keep on walking but he runs over to her, as if he hasn't seen a living soul for weeks. He jumps in front of her on the pavement, panting for breath. He looks bad.

"Hi, Vincent."

"Beauty." He kisses her on the cheeks. He smells of alcohol.

"How was your *Streetcar* received?"

"Haven't you read about it?"

"I don't keep up with all that, Vin."

"No, why would you."

"Well?"

"Very decently, very decently. Except by you-know-who." He pulls a strange face and gives her a cross-eyed look as he says it, probably in imitation of you-know-who. "But in fact that's a compliment." She has no idea who he's talking about. "Almost forgotten about it already. Started on something new."

"Chekhov, wasn't it?"

"That's later, next season. No, you definitely need to see that. No, a little thing, a little thing, a minor directing job with a young cast."

"What play?"

"They're so young, Emilia. Early twenties. And they're so nice. So much nicer than I was. And more civilized, far less radical. Is that pure chance?" His face adopts a panicky expression. He's taken hold of her arm.

"I don't know, Vincent."

"And they're so beautiful, so lively, so, so ... And they don't realize it, not at all, they drink water and eat salad, Emilia. They're so ... They have no idea. It's driving me mad."

"What is, Vin?"

"That I'm so old, that I'm so sodding old."

"You're not old."

"Compared to them I am. I'm old. And they're young and don't even know."

"Youth is wasted on the young."

"That's true, that's really true. Wilde?"

"Shaw."

"You're an exceptional woman."

"Don't act the fool."

"I *am* a fool. That's the truth. But you're not. You're someone who can keep a secret. And that's incredible."

What kind of talk is this? She needs to get away from here. Soon she'll never be rid of him. If someone tells you a secret, you become partly responsible and can't just take to your heels. He's grabbed hold of her arm. He looks as though he's about to pour his heart out.

"Emilia."

"Chin up, Vincent, stay strong. Theatre isn't everything, right?" She turns up her collar.

"No, I guess not, I guess not. Okay. Say hi to Bruch."

She tries to remember whether Vincent has a girlfriend at the moment, whether there's anyone she ought to send greetings to. He continues to stand there, as motionless as those willows in the meadow, while she moves away from him.

Josepha has thick blonde hair and a sleepy face. Her small eyes are wide apart and her mouth is big. There's something sensual about her, with that mouth and the languid way she moves. Although it's only early afternoon, they've ordered wine. Eddy comes into the café. He doesn't look particularly broken. He immediately corrects them: Marieke hasn't pressed charges, she's merely reported it to the police, which has no further consequences. Eddy orders *bitterballen*. And there's that email to all the staff in which she describes the times that he went and stood right up against her, the remarks, the invitations, and ultimately the assault at the end of the day after everyone had left. How he kissed her and touched her all over and how, petrified and unable to do anything, she endured it.

"So is all of that true?" Josepha asks.

Eddy shrugs, says an accusation of sexual assault is quite often the mould into which a girl pours her regret. That he hadn't for a moment got the impression she wasn't enjoying it. Josepha asks him how likely it is that one of the others, former staff members or former interns, will add an episode to the story.

"No chance," says Eddy, exclaiming that they know him, don't they?

"We certainly do," says Emilia. "Precisely."

At that Eddy is deeply offended. "I'm a virile man, not a brute."

"You should keep your hands off the interns."

"Even when there's mutual consent? And only off the interns?"

"Jesus, Eddy, come on, cut your losses. Apologize,

hand Marieke over to me, take a week off, talk to the staff. Admit you were wrong." As she's talking, Josepha makes a brushing gesture over the tabletop, as if trying to sweep the subject away.

"Eddy."

Eddy sighs.

"Emilia."

"Have you ever raped anyone?" She's looked up the statistics. Every day, four rapes are registered in the Netherlands and many times that number go unreported. She hasn't been able to find any figures at all for the percentage of men who rape, or the average number of rapes per rapist. "I don't mean that murky grey area where opinions differ. Have you ever actually, against the wishes of the woman you were lying on top of ..."

"No, of course not." His voice sounds loud and flat and he isn't even looking at her. Is he shocked by her suggestion, or is he lying?

"We're your friends. Wouldn't it be nice, interesting, just to lay all your sins on the table?"

"Emil, shut up." Josepha looks at her, frowning. "Come on now, stop."

"I mean it. It happens, doesn't it? About ten times a day, if not more. And somebody does it, right? Wouldn't it be interesting if we could have a conversation on the subject? Wouldn't that be progressive?"

"But what if there's no conversation to be had? What if I've never raped anyone?"

"But you have sexually assaulted someone."

"Without knowing it!"

"Do you think it's normal for a person to be petrified while they put up with you touching them?"

93

"I never noticed she was petrified. I didn't notice!"

"So what did you notice?"

"I thought she was nervous, that she was too young and inexperienced, too ... too blown away ... by me ... I thought maybe she was still a virgin. I stopped, because I thought maybe she was still a virgin, and that seemed like going too far, I only wanted to ... as two adults together. I sent her away then. I think that's what ... what made her angry. That she felt rejected. That it's completely the opposite of what she claims. I think she's in love with me. But I'll deny it all, guys, all of it, because of Yildiz."

All three of them are silent. The *bitterballen* arrive.

"I believe this. I believe you. What about you, Emilia?" Josepha orders a fresh round of drinks. Emilia wonders whether it's possible to have a real conversation, with anyone, a real, frank conversation. About what happens to you, about what you do wrong, about what you think, about what you don't normally dare to say. What would that be worth? Is it interesting? Would Eddy's secret inner life really interest her? You probably get to know people just as well from the ways they hide themselves.

"So you believe him. And does it make sense to you that he believes her immobility was love and admiration? Oh yes, and lack of experience? If that's his defence, then his claim that he's never raped anyone is meaningless. Maybe he didn't notice?"

"Does the possibility exist in your world that Marieke made it all up?"

Emilia thinks about that for a moment. Then she shakes her head. That possibility is out of the question.

"The whole moral outcry," Eddy snorts. "That 'you should keep your hands off the interns.' As if Marieke isn't an adult, for God's sake; as if we aren't two grown-ups who can say yes and no! I mean, I didn't drug her or tie her up or beat her to a pulp. I swear I'm telling the truth. Do you believe me?"

"It doesn't matter. Does it?"

Towards six o'clock Emilia rings Bruch. They decide to forgive Alicia for the whisky transgression so that they've got a babysitter. She stays in Amsterdam.

Chapter 11

BRUCH HAD OPENED the window. The streetlights hanging from cables strung across the street swayed in the wind and lit up the rain beneath. He hadn't asked about her absence. She hadn't said anything about it. He cooked. She found an Italian language course in the bookcase, loaded one of the cassette tapes, and repeated the lines. They named all the countries they'd been to. They named all the countries they wanted to visit. He talked about his patients and she talked about her company, the SOS. He made tea. They made love again. He made love to her without dropping that watchful gaze. He looked at her body while he was touching it. He looked at her face while he entered her. He kissed her eyelids and licked her lips. "You're moaning," he said when she moaned. He fell asleep. She studied his face. After that, she too went to sleep and when she woke he was looking at her. He made coffee and fetched the newspaper.

"I arrived at that party of Jacob's when it was almost over. You tried to blow the snow out of my hair and insisted on putting an icicle in my drink. It seems you'd all done that earlier in the evening, but the edge of the roof was empty and you slipped on the balcony. You were fairly drunk. But you had a beautiful bright glow in your eyes. I thought Jacob was your boyfriend. I got talking with someone in the kitchen. I stood there tossing back drinks because I'd arrived completely sober at a party where everyone was already bombed. I got into a blinding row about dressage, a ridiculous subject that I don't understand at all. When I came into the living room you were lying on your back, on the floor, in between your two brothers, listening to atrocious psychedelic music. I stood looking at the three of you for a bit. Then I left."

"With someone?"

"With someone, yes."

"Someone you'd never met until that evening?"

"Correct."

"And never saw again after that."

"Almost."

"Only a few times."

"Only a few times ..."

"But when we saw each other at the hospital six months later you recognized me immediately."

"Yes."

"Because you'd been thinking about me all that time."

"No."

"You're supposed to say yes. For the story."

"Yes."

"So no, then?"

"No."

"You'd forgotten about me. But when you saw me you remembered that bright glowing look of mine and the purpose of your life."

"And you didn't recognize me at all, but that felt as if you'd forgotten something very important."

"Yes."

They talked endlessly about those first meetings, reconstructing their thoughts, imagining possible variations, sharpening their memories, polishing them into glorious confirmation. Emilia believed it underlined the correctness of her decision to keep quiet about what had happened to her. He would never talk to her with such insouciance or let himself go in her arms like that if he knew.

Later, she thought. When everything's back to normal. When we know each other and what's happened can't soil me in his eyes. Then I'll tell him.

They went to bars and they lay in bed. They told each other about their lives, their childhoods, their work. He got up early to go for a run. She made coffee and fossicked through his things. She found postcards from his ex, Mariette. Even the smallest details of his life—annotations in a book, the start of a letter to a friend whose name hadn't yet come up in his stories, a loose photo, a pebble he'd kept—made her feel she was penetrating deeper into him.

Bruch changed jobs. Emilia gave up her room and moved in with him. Although they both worked a lot, it was as if they had endless time for each other. They no longer walked through the city so much. They went to the cinema, enjoyed sitting in bars imagining what the people around them did, fashioning them into characters. They went on holiday together for the first time, to Italy, and decided to marry. He introduced her to his parents, intelligent, standoffish people who made her part of the family without any hesitation but without much warmth either. She met his sister, Philippa, with whom he had a difficult relationship, not because of anything that had happened but because of irreconcilable temperaments. She'd been converted to Christianity and according to Bruch it had magnified all the dogmatic, superficial, condemnatory tendencies in her character. Emilia told Bruch about the death of her mother. As for her father, she said only that there was a rift that could never be repaired.

The first argument they had was about Jacob. Bruch said it wasn't normal, the way he behaved with her. An angry exchange arose over the question of what was normal, and whether you could use "not normal" as an argument at all—as if there was such a thing as normal, as if there was a norm that Bruch personally knew to be right.

"He's your brother!"

"You don't say!"

"The way he touches you! The way he puts his paws on you. In my house."

"In my house."

"In our house. It's not normal."

"There you go again! Are you the great determiner of norms, Bruch? We're close. He's my big brother. He's all I've got."

"Jesus!"

"Apart from you."

"Jesus!!"

"As far as family goes."

"Pathetic!"

"Apart from Viktor. Who's no use to me."

"He ignores me when he's here."

"You're jealous! How stupid! How ugly! I'm going out."

He stopped her. They both brought it to a head. She said he was disgusting, acting like this.

"What am I supposed to think?"

"Something else, something more intelligent."

"About you!?"

"Whatever you like. That's what you do anyway, right?"

He gave her a slap. Then she gave him a slap. After that they stood looking at each other, bewildered.

"Ow," she said, after a pause. He burst out laughing. She gave him another slap. He grabbed her wrists and they horsed around and collapsed in giggles. Until he was suddenly sitting on top of her, holding her arms above her head with one hand as he started to stroke her body with the other hand. Then she vomited. He let her go and moved away from her. She struggled upright and knelt there puking on the carpet. He didn't say anything. She didn't say anything either. He cleaned the floor while she lay curled up in bed.

Chapter 12

AFTER GRADUATING IN medicine, Jacob told Viktor and Emilia that he wanted to become a psychiatrist. Viktor fell off his chair laughing.

"Don't you need, er, empathy for that?"

Jacob retorted that he wasn't going to become a social therapist, that it was still a branch of medicine.

"And incidentally, my interaction with people including my unhinged little brother has given me a kindhearted view of humanity."

"Your unhinged little brother?"

"Yes. Look at you sitting there with your drooping shoulders and your inward gaze." They'd fought, half for fun, and half for Viktor, to prove that although he wasn't a man of Jacob's magnitude, he made up for it in passion. Viktor had already spent three years studying a different subject each year. He wanted a broad education, he said, and wasn't interested in a career. He worked at an anarchist radio station. He spoilt all their evenings with his urge to argue. Emilia was sixteen at the time and still living at home. She visited Jacob every other week, fitting seamlessly into the life he led. On the Sunday evening she would sit in the train home with a hangover, exhausted but recharged.

"Mercy, mercy," Jacob roared, to humour Viktor.

They trawl through those memories at the huge table in the vast kitchen of the enormous house that Jacob and Lieke live in. The doors to the garden are open, the rain is tipping down, and the sky is an improbably dark grey. Everything about Jacob is big: his head, his hands, his ears, his arms, his belly. He radiates a coarse sort of stoutness. His hair is brown with a red sheen. He has a probing, arrogant gaze, which scares people who don't know him and means that his patients have to overcome a degree of timidity before they reveal themselves, but also that ultimately they don't dare lie to him.

On the kitchen counter, four large slices of salmon are waiting for the gathering to be complete.

"Didn't Dad ever ask what we got up to in Amsterdam at weekends?" Jacob asks.

"I wasn't speaking to him in those days."

"But later you did, right?"

"Later I did, yes."

"And then you stopped again."

"Yes."

"And now?"

"It no longer matters. He doesn't recognize anyone. He has no memory. He's forgotten everything."

"I thought it was an act. To make it all go away."

"Did you really think that?"

"Yes."

"He's got Korsakoff's Syndrome. I thought you knew."

"I don't know anything. But never mind. I don't need to know."

She stands up and lingers next to the sink. She sticks her finger into some soft cheese and strokes the fish's pink flesh.

"Get a knife if you like. And a serving board."

She opens the fridge and inspects the contents. There are only expensive things in it. Jacob and Lieke do their daily shopping at the delicatessen.

"Have you ever treated a rapist?"

"Has it ever struck you that our conversations often resemble interviews?"

"No. Really?"

"Yes, I have."

"And?"

"What do you want to know?"

"The motive."

"Anger, mostly. Hatred of women. Sexual deviance, sometimes. Sadism, occasionally."

"And yours?"

"Anger. Poor impulse control."

"Can I open that champagne?"

"Of course. Put another one in to cool. There, behind that door."

"Did it trouble him?"

"Trouble?"

"Yes, you only treat people who're suffering, right? Was he sorry?"

"Maybe. Yes. Maybe he was. He was depressed. For a while I worked one day a week in the jail. A completely pointless invention."

She starts smearing soft stinky cheese on crackers.

"Because it makes rapists depressed."

"It makes everyone depressed, or angry, depending

on their temperament. It's an incredibly stupid environment. It kills you inside. And it doesn't help."

"What should we do with criminals, then?" Viktor stands dripping in the doorway.

"Forgive them. Mostly. And help. If possible. I assume you regard an umbrella as a bourgeois accoutrement? Em, grab a towel from that cupboard. Over there. Not one step inside, you!"

"Unbelievable how everyone does exactly what you say." Emilia drapes the towel over Viktor's wet head and kisses his wet cheeks. He strips to his underwear and then comes indoors.

"Brudders!" He raises a fist in the air.

"In arms!" Emilia too. Jacob doesn't join in.

"Who's the criminal?"

"Nobody." Emilia gives each of her brothers a glass.

"Can a person who's angry be depressed?"

"Depression is anger turned inwards."

"Is that so?"

"It's what I think."

"Is that a theory of yours?"

"I think that's how it is."

"You say prison makes people depressed." Viktor's tone promises a lengthy exposition.

"Or angry."

"Or angry, but I think the whole system we live in …"

"Are you now going to say this society is a prison?"

"I was intending to use rather more words."

"Is that a theory of yours?"

"Not of mine in particular."

Jacob lets his head fall to the table with a bump.

"Jesus, Jake, how infuriating you are!"

"Em," Jacob asks her, "did I ever tell you about Vik's tree campaign?"

"No."

"No?"

"No!"

"Really? So I never told you how at the party when our primary school had been in existence for however many years and everyone was invited to come in fancy dress and we paraded through the village, Viktor—aged seven he was, at most—came dressed as a tree? With a notice board and a stick, and in the scrawl he'd only just mastered he'd daubed *Acid rain, I can't stand it anymore*."

"It wasn't a party," Viktor says. "It was a demonstration. Against acid rain. That was a thing in those days. You thought it was a party, you thought everything was a party, as in a reason to drink."

Jacob is putting crackers with Époisses into his mouth as if they're popcorn.

"So everyone went as cowboys or indians or fairies or I don't know what, but Vikkie here went as a weeping willow." Viktor grabs the towel, which is still round his neck, and flings it at Jacob.

"You're remembering it all wrong. You've tangled that whole period together, friend. Emilia, say something, you were only about five but you've got a good memory. Compared to Jacob, at least."

Emilia lets a teasingly long silence fall in which she continues to look at Viktor.

"You've got a girlfriend, I'm told."

"Yes. Olga. Here." He shows her a photo on his phone. "Okay, Jacob. I'll stop. Not because you asked me but because there's no point arguing with you two."

"Right. That's what I'm saying."

Then Lieke comes in, small, fine-featured, elegant, ten years older than Jacob. She kisses Jacob as if they're alone. Emilia briefly stares at his big hands on her slim back. Then Lieke carefully wipes the lipstick off his face and turns to look at them.

"Emilia, sweetheart, it's been ages!"

"Lieke, you look dazzling."

"Viktor!" She kisses him then turns back to Emilia. "Aren't you having any problems there with the water? I heard on the news that the rivers are really high."

"Not yet," Emilia mumbles. She plays with the cat. Lieke talks about a case of suicide that turned out to be murder and the cat purrs and the rain falls and Emilia imagines that her whole life is a dream.

When Viktor has gone to Olga, and Lieke to bed, Emilia lies on the sofa with her feet in Jacob's hands. He slides his fists along the soles of her feet and pinches her heels. Then he strokes her calves.

"Do you think Vik's happy?" she asks.

"Yes."

"Or do you think that's a silly question?"

"No, why?"

"How can you know whether someone's happy?"

"You just keep the definition simple."

"Isn't it complicated by definition?"

"What is happiness?"

"This. Being here like this?"

"Yes?" He pinches her foot hard.

"Is it A: a feeling of oneness, of equilibrium and the certainty that nothing can disturb the balance."

"Yes?"

"Or B: a sense of oneness, of equilibrium and the certainty that the whole thing could fall to pieces at any moment?"

"Got any cigarettes?"

"In my bag."

"Want more wine?"

She holds up her glass. He fills it.

"Which is it for you?"

She thinks for a few seconds. She's a bit dizzy.

"C."

"Something else, namely, dotted line."

"A sense of being free of all thoughts."

"Ah, right."

"Something physical."

"For me happiness is the feeling that I'm floating above a landscape like an eagle, concentrating fiercely, noticing everything below me, seeing everything, able to strike at any moment, with pinpoint accuracy."

"And for Lieke?"

"Lieke just wants everything to be beautiful."

"What?"

"Forget it."

They smoke in the doorway to the garden. It's still raining. Emilia contemplates Lieke's remark about water. She picks up her phone. Bruch has sent photos of the attic and of the empty wall where the kitchen used to be. His message simply says, *Had chips with the boys.*

"Did you expect me not to start a family?"

"That's a strange question."

"Really?"

"It's not what I expected."

"You thought I'd stay with you."

"Maybe I didn't actually expect you ever to grow up."

"Now that really is strange."

"I wanted to protect you from everything when you were little. I didn't want you to be influenced by anything, not by that pathetic school, or by those people, that stale perspective on everything that was instilled into us. Do you have that with your children? The feeling you're delivering them up to the world, to the system, as Viktor would say?"

She thinks about a group of parents that came to the sos to commission a study into the right to individualized education, an elite group wanting to shore up its elitist position even further. She pictures Leo in front of her. Clever, quiet, seeking a position for himself.

"The most heartbreaking to me is the urge to adapt, to command whatever's normal. The will to survive, to become someone, a person who does well, in the teacher's eyes, to become someone who resembles someone else ... That complete lack of sophistication that children have, which means you can so clearly see it happening."

They are silent for a moment.

"I've done it all wrong with Bruch. I've done it completely wrong. And now this is it. Now this is what we are. I have to go home, Jacob. I can't stay."

"You're a bit drunk, I think."

"Not that drunk."

"Get into bed with me. First sleep for a bit."

"Doesn't Lieke sleep there?"

"Sometimes."

"Maybe I'll have to get divorced. Maybe I'll simply have to leave. Maybe I just can't do it."

"Come on, I'll take you there, I'll lay you down."

She looks at his face, which resembles her face. Her eyes keep falling shut, but every time she opens them he's looking at her. She tries to tell a riddle about three brothers and seventeen camels, but she loses the thread.

Chapter 13

LIEKE SLIPS INTO the room and puts a tray on the low cupboard against the wall. She's wearing a white suit. Emilia peers at her with the eye closest to the pillow and keeps the other eye shut. She doesn't move. The smell of coffee. It takes her a while to realize that Jacob has gone. Minutes later she hears the sound of the front door being pulled shut. Then she pushes the quilt aside and goes to the window. Beyond the curtains, which let in beige light, and beyond the balcony, lies the street. The sky is a dirty grey. The gardens below look wet, deserted, and neglected. Lieke comes out of the shed and looks up before getting on her bicycle. They wave to each other. "And there she goes," Emilia says aloud, "to pass judgement." She drinks her coffee standing by the cupboard. There's orange juice too, and a croissant of which she eats only the crusty tips. There are two missed messages from Bruch, but when she rings back he doesn't pick up. She gets dressed. She opens the wardrobe and looks at Jacob's clothes. His professionally folded shirts are in tall, neat piles. His suits hang motionless on their hangers. She rummages through his drawers until she finds Valium and puts the little box in her pocket. She leafs through the books on the bedside table: all specialist literature. Then she searches on her phone for information about current water levels. On the water authority website she reads that the risk of flooding in her postcode district is greater than one in a hundred. It doesn't say how much greater. She can't even find out whether a higher risk category exists. This website is so user-friendly that it's impossible to get any information not directly relevant to you.

In the kitchen, music is playing very softly. She wants to turn it off but can't see a CD player or anything like it anywhere, nor can she find the source of the sound. There's a remote control on the table, but when she points it upwards and presses a button the light goes off. None of the buttons will turn the light back on. She makes another cup of coffee and contemplates the term "devastating flooding." She lies on the floor and concentrates on her breathing. She needs to ring Josepha. That time, already a year ago maybe, when Eddy asked her to keep track of her hours—that's when she should have resigned. The tragedy of every departure is that it comes too late. It's suddenly getting very dark in the room. When she turns her head she sees bad weather approaching in the thick cloud covering. Can regret be an inherited tendency? Can an awareness of mortality hit you like an avalanche? She must persuade Bruch to emigrate; they need to start again somewhere else. While they still can. Her telephone rings. The river is pouring over the jetty and across the garden. But the house is dry. He's delivered the boys as normal. While they're talking the rain starts again.

"I'm off to work. Are you coming home?"

"Yes."

"Then I'll cancel Alicia."

"Yes."

"Is everything okay?"

"How d'you mean?"

"With you?"

Her voice can no longer get past her throat. She tries to breathe in through her ears. Could she tell him now what she didn't tell him then, as if it's only just happened? Could she simply nullify the time between? Because all time, once it passes, seems to have disappeared. Because it's only now that she wants to tell someone what it was like to think she was going to die.

"Emilia?"

"Yes."

"Just come home now."

"Right." She hangs up. She rubs her throat. The rain lays a misty filter on the glass doors. She can't make out individual drops; the water moves down the window as one body. Her thoughts are both unspecific and unstoppable. She waits until she has her breathing back under control, then stands up and walks to the hallway to get her coat. Here too, music is coming out of the ceiling. How ridiculous is that? So Jacob has a house that makes music? A house that plays piano softly while you're away? Through a small window in the side wall she sees someone on the path, approaching the house. In a reflex she presses herself to the wall. He rings the bell. She hopes he won't put his face to the glass to look in, because then there's a chance he'll see her. After a second ring of the bell, the letterbox clatters.

She waits a few minutes just to make sure, then slips back into the kitchen, goes upstairs to the room at the front, and looks down at the street. As far as she can see, there's no longer anyone there. As far as she can tell, nobody is hiding behind the hedge. She's now in Lieke's room. It has the same impersonal cheerfulness as Jacob's, the same antique Empire furniture, the same pure white cover on the bed. In front of the oval mirror are countless bottles and pots. Emilia stares at them for a while and feels the little rectangular box of pills in her pocket. She takes out two small blue pills and looks at them lying in her hand. She puts them in her mouth and drains the glass next to the bed. It's only then that it occurs to her she has to drive. It'll be half an hour before they start to take effect and, if she hurries, the busiest part of the trip will be behind her by then. She goes downstairs, puts on her coat, and packs her bag. She peers along the empty pavement before opening the door. The moment she pulls the door shut, she realizes that her phone is still on the kitchen counter.

The news starts and finishes with the flooding. Some streets are underwater, a roof has caved in under the weight of the rain, and people are interviewed about their flooded cellars, about their sodden belongings. She turns off the radio and slides the Brahms string sextet into the CD player.

She once listened to a man in New Orleans whose wine cellar was flooded after Katrina. The wine, worth tens of thousands of euros per bottle, bought at auctions, was intact, safe inside the glass, but the labels had been soaked off so it was worthless. Naked bottles floated around between scraps of illegible paper: no better way to underline how meaningless and mendacious his business was. You paid sixty thousand euros for a label and nobody would recognize the supposed value of the wine if they tasted it. "We can throw all this away," said the wine trader. "Or drink it," suggested the woman interviewing him. "Which comes down to the same thing," he said.

She turns onto the ring road, and while Brahms's strings climb higher and higher she makes good speed. The damp chill of the rain outside disappears from the car and it grows warm, comfortable. The sky is the same asphalt grey as the road surface. She has to force herself to keep her eyes on the road and not lose herself in the metronomic sweep of the windscreen wipers.

She rejects as absurd the still sparkling idea of telling it as if it happened yesterday. She'll have to come to terms with having said nothing. You can't undo a thing like that. At best you can say that all those years ago you didn't say ... et cetera. It won't be possible to get now what she could have got then: consolation, vicarious anger, treatment. It'll be all about why she kept quiet rather than about the event itself. It'll be about the question of why she's telling the story now, all of a sudden, about what's wrong with her now that's making her tell it. Bruch might even become irritated, as if she's deploying a disproportionately drastic means of getting his attention. To the question about her life in the present—about what makes her want to start talking about that time now—she doesn't have an answer. When she tries to remember how she's been over the past few years, she tumbles into a misty void. Has she been happy? Dynamic? Gloomy? She has no idea. Where was she? What does it mean that she can't remember anything about the past year? Was she happy? Is that it?

A loud honking catapults her out of her thoughts and back onto the road. She skews the crash barrier out of her windscreen just in time. A silhouette taps aggressively at his forehead then races on ahead. Not until the road is central once more, straight in front of her and shiny with rain, do the nerves billow in her stomach. Almost dead. Slowly, in the right-hand lane, without Brahms now, she drives on to the next petrol station. She parks at the most secluded spot, turns off the engine, tilts the seat back, and shuts her eyes. Which do you choose? By fire or by flood? No arms or no legs? Dead or your child dead? Overwhelmed by heat or by cold? The rain drums on the roof. The highway murmurs like the sea. On the inside of her eyelids an image of a bowl of porridge appears, its elastic skin briefly offering resistance to a piece of fruit laid on top before taking it in and closing over it. She falls asleep.

Chapter 14

AS SOON AS she turns into their road, Bruch storms out. He stops about twenty metres in front of the car. The rain turns the shoulders of his shirt from light to dark blue. She switches off the engine and continues to look at him. From this distance she can't make out his facial expression.

She woke up an hour ago. Her leg had gone to sleep; her neck felt stiff and painful. She couldn't see anything through the misted-up windows and for a few seconds she was completely disorientated. For one heart-stopping moment she thought she was driving. She grabbed the wheel with a shriek and rubbed a gap in the condensation on the windscreen with her sleeve. Then she saw the verge, the litter bin, the picnic table, the view of an empty meadow, the trucks. The whole dreary scene. She gasped and rubbed her neck, remembering the near accident, the Valium. She thought of her brothers, of that acid-rain story, of Viktor in his underpants. A fuzzy interlacing of love, regret, and sadness enveloped her. A quarter to four. She was supposed to pick up the boys. She was supposed to have picked up the boys. She got out for a couple of minutes, moving to wake her stiff body, letting the rain refresh her face. Then she drove on, calmly, since there was no way to make up the time. She left the highway and drove the last fifteen kilometres on minor roads. Water splashed up from the wheels, trees that normally lined the riverbank now rose out of the water. One barn was standing photogenically in the midst of the current. A helicopter flew over the wet land, surely not by chance.

Why is he just standing there? Behind him the open door, the yellow light, the promise of warmth. Is Bruch an obstacle? She gets out.

"Where have you been?"

"Where are the boys?"

"Inside. Why aren't you answering your phone?"

"Who fetched them?"

"I did. I got a call at the hospital."

"Sorry."

"Are you all right?"

"I don't know. Shouldn't we go in?"

"You're suddenly in a hurry now?"

"We're getting wet."

"What's the matter with you?"

"Can I get past?"

"No." His whole shirt is dark blue now. His hair is dripping. A drop of water hangs from his earlobe. "Where were you?"

"The truth?"

"Please!"

"I'd taken Valium before I got into the car. Then I nearly had an accident. I was sitting in a parking spot to recover when I fell asleep. I woke up five hours later. My phone's at Jacob's place." The truth. He looks at her, squeezes his eyes shut. "You don't believe me."

"You're behaving strangely."

"Sorry."

"For ages now."

"Yes."

"What's the matter?"

"I'm going to leave the sos."

"Because of Eddy?"

"No. Yes. That too. I don't know. I've had enough."

"How did you get hold of the pills?"

"From Jacob."

"He gave them to you?"

"I took them. It's only Valium, Bruch, not heroin!"

"Emilia."

"Oh, right, you know that, of course. You're a doctor." That look of his. She walks past him, pushing his arm away when he reaches out towards her.

He grabs her by the shoulder and says "Ho!" as if she's an animal.

"Goddammit Emilia, talk to me!"

Leo and Osip are watching television. She slips past the door unseen and dashes up the stairs. Once there, she doesn't know what to do. She hears the front door slam. Hard. She peels off her wet clothes and looks out. The garden has been partly claimed by the river, which has won terrain from the meadows on the far bank as well. The river is at least three times as wide as normal. Posts, trees, bushes, the fence around the cows on the far side—everything is sticking up out of the water. Through the binoculars they keep next to the window she looks for the bank, for where the river stops now, but can't determine where that is. Raindrops punch holes in the mirror, a thousand silent water craters.

"Dinner!" Bruch shouts up the stairs. She pulls herself away from the view and puts on some clothes. Downstairs they're already sitting at the table, plates in front of them. The kitchen has been installed. It gleams. Bruch has made meatballs.

"Mummy!"

She avoids Bruch's eyes.

"Karin let me sit with her in the office. She gave me a picture to colour in." Karin is the school receptionist. Leo is afraid of her. Emilia strokes his wrist and says nothing. Osip squashes his potato flat with his hand. He squeals because it's hot. Bruch bundles him under his arm and holds his hand under the high, shiny new tap. Leo looks at Emilia, upwards at an angle with his face close to his plate, almost embarrassed, or at any rate shy.

"Are you ill, Mum?" She shakes her head. There's something congealed, something leaden, something immobile inside her. She was about ten years old. Her mother was slumped in a chair at the table, ill. Her father silently ate everything on his plate. Jacob fired facts at them, like a quizmaster in a quiz with drugged contestants. What does BMW stand for? Which plant that grows in the school playground will kill you if you take just one bite? Which planet is the hottest? What was Stalin's favourite food?

"No, love. I'm not ill."

"Are you angry?"

"No sweetie, not angry, not with you, don't be silly."

Osip wants to sit on her lap, but Bruch says he can't. "Eat first. And let your mother eat first too."

But Emilia says, "Oh never mind, it's okay, just for a moment, just this once, come on then." He folds himself against her and stuffs his hands into the neck of her jumper, under her clothes. He presses his wet mouth to her cheek. Bruch looks at them crossly. No sitting on laps at the table is the rule. First eat and then play is the rule. In the past, a decade ago, before she knew him, before she started on all this, she was aware of it, but somehow or other she forgot, having fallen in love, in the grip of existence, longing for these children. Now here it lies again in its full glory, stretched out before her: bottled-up feelings, unexpressed thoughts. The children are still small, but there too it's already started; secrets are already brewing inside them. The parents can't talk in the presence of the children, the children can't talk in the presence of the parents. And the parents can't talk to each other, for that matter. A family is a mould for pouring your happiness into, to give it a solid shape. It's a way of reconciling yourself to the banality of things. A prison you can safely lock yourself up in.

"If you want pudding, Osip, then you'll go and sit on your own chair." Bruch is intent on making an issue out of it.

"I want pudding."

"Then go and sit on your own chair."

"I don't want to sit on my chair."

"Then you won't get any pudding."

"I want pudding."

"Then go and sit on your own chair, Osip."

"I want to sit with Mummy!"

"If you want pudding, you'll have to go and sit on

your chair. Afterwards you can sit with Mummy again. Come on."

"No-o-o."

"Okay."

"Pudding."

"No, sweetheart, that means no pudding."

"Pudding!"

"Osip."

"Mummy! Pudding!"

"You have to sit on your chair, Os." Leo tries to salvage the situation. Emilia wants to disappear. But this meal has to be finished, then the children need to be bathed, put to bed, the whole ritual that she won't be able to get out of, not after everything that's happened today. Then she'll have to talk to Bruch. She can see him keeping his anger burning, there on the other side of the table. Osip goes to sit on his chair and eats his pudding, crying. Emilia is unable to move.

She puréed vegetables, spread syrup on soft, crustless white bread, took a thermos of tea upstairs twice a day, and emptied the bucket. Her mother's face was contorted with pain; later the morphine made it soft and distant. Sometimes she ranted in her delirium. Emilia made no effort to decipher a message in it. She was only at home until she could get away. She ate dinner each day with her father. He asked routine questions, about school, about what she was planning to do that evening. She gave answers that consisted of single words, or a few at best. She was going out with a boy from the village. They spent after-school hours on his narrow bed in a house that was as quiet as hers. They had sex and played computer games. The nurses who came to the house made just as much effort as she did to be done with their tasks as quickly as possible and leave again. For the final few weeks, her mother was in hospital in a nearby town. Emilia went with her father every other day. They sat at the bedside and said nothing. On the windowsill were withered flowers. Her father said everything was pointless. Her mother no longer spoke. Then she died. There were people at the funeral Emilia had never seen before and they painted a picture of a woman she'd never known. Two months later, a week after her seventeenth birthday, she moved out.

She reads to the children, helps them brush their teeth, and puts them to bed. Her silence induces compliance. So that's how it works. They're afraid and seem good. She's inherited her parents' motion-lessness. She understands what it is, what that external stasis does. She understands it but can't manage to analyse it fully. She can't get her thoughts into focus and feels trapped. There's a lack of oxygen in the room. She wants to go outside. She wants to leave. When she goes downstairs, Bruch is standing in the doorway looking at the wet garden. The rain is still falling. The gleaming new kitchen makes it seem as if she's in a different house from her own. She sits at the table and waits. She decides to give as sincere and detailed an answer to each of Bruch's questions as possible. If he asks her again what she's hiding, she'll tell him everything. She'll just talk, even if she doesn't know where it will end. Her heart beats in her throat. Everything. No more secrets and no more stasis. If he asks her to, she'll turn herself inside out.

"Emilia."

"Yes," she says, solemnly. Yes to everything, she thinks.

"I have to go out for a bit."

"What?"

"I'm off for a while."

"Where to?"

"Just out."

"Okay."

"Okay?"

"Yes."

He shuts the French windows, looks at her, for no more than a second, then turns round and leaves the kitchen, and the house. The car crunches over the gravel of the driveway. She shouldn't have agreed. She shouldn't have waited for the question. She must keep off the whisky.

Chapter 15

A WOMAN FROM the local council has been round. She said that asking them to leave the house was merely advice for the time being. But at a later stage it might become an order. Bruch and Emilia stand in the garden, boots in the water. Bruch has fetched sandbags and sheets of stiff plastic. He's nailed up the cellar window and sealed the bottoms of the doorways. It's still raining. Emilia's car has water halfway up the wheels. Bruch left his up on the road when he came back after taking the boys.

"I'm not leaving here," he said. "I live here."

"Yes."

"What will they do if the evacuation becomes compulsory and we refuse to leave?"

"I think in cases like that they call in the army."

Emilia hasn't been helping. She's watched him hauling the last of the sand and stacking the sandbags against the back wall. He carried things upstairs and put food into boxes. Leo was thrilled and wanted to go to school by boat.

"It's not that bad yet," Bruch said.

"But when it is that bad, can I go to school by boat?"

"Yes."

"What boat?" Emilia asked.

"We've got a rubber dinghy, haven't we? I do believe we've got a rubber dinghy somewhere. Perhaps you could go and look for it." She went inside then but she didn't look for the boat. She looked at the damp patches appearing on the floor of the conservatory close to the walls, at the kitchen, at the gleaming red cupboard doors, at the wooden skirting below them, at the immeasurable space on the countertop. She opened and shut drawers that glided soundlessly, like tongues stuck out and withdrawn, and looked inside them, where everything was clean and arranged so neatly that she barely recognized any of it.

"Emilia!" Bruch was standing in front of her. "Can't you hear me?"

"No, sorry."

"Help me for a bit, okay?"

"Okay."

She has to hold a plank while he drives screws into it. She doesn't understand how sheets of stiff plastic against wooden doors could keep the water out. She hasn't got a decent raincoat; the water dribbles down her back. Does he know that the floor in there is already wet?

"Shall we go indoors for a while? Shall I make coffee?"

"Hold that straight please." There's no hope left. They're saving their house, not their marriage. "Is it so very difficult? Come on!"

"I don't feel good."

"Just a little longer."

She holds the plank straight. The fact that it's such a simple task is what makes it complicated. It's too small to concentrate on; her mind keeps slipping off.

"Okay. Forget it. Just go inside." He says it in a supposedly neutral voice. She goes into the kitchen and drops her coat on the floor. Her clothes are wet. She makes coffee. Her heart is beating too fast. The doorbell rings. She looks outside to see whether Bruch has heard, but he's bent over with his hood up, wielding a hammer. She sticks a potato knife into the back pocket of her jeans and walks to the hall. It's the postman, with a package. He's wearing rubber boots with his trouser legs stuffed into them. She sees him glance at her wet clothes. He makes an attempt to look past her into the house. Asks how they're doing, whether they're managing to stay dry. She says everything's fine and shuts the door in his face. Why does she live in a village? Why does she live in a village like she used to? In a village where the postman knows all the neighbours and the neighbours are always in need of a chat. In the package is her phone with a note from Jacob. *Look after yourself little one. If you need me to come and get you, I'll come.* Bruch steps inside. Without saying anything he picks up her coat from the floor and hangs it over a chair. He hangs his own waterproofs on the catch of the window above the back door and puts a floorcloth underneath. He pours coffee and gives her a cup.

"Have you got flu?" Flu is a lack of enthusiasm, a tutor at university once said to her when she reported sick.

"I don't know."

"What have you got?"

"I don't know, obviously."

"But perhaps you can tell me what the problem is. Have you got a fever? Are you in pain? Are you dizzy?" The irritation slows his speech, as if putting on the brakes is the only way he can prevent himself from shouting at her. She'll have to make something up. It doesn't have to be true. She can just say she feels nauseous and dizzy. Then she can go upstairs and lie down. It would be good to sleep. She was awake all night. She looked at Osip and Leo as they slept, aware of the fragility of their lives, of the possibility that a life can derail completely. She looked at Bruch and thought: I know you, don't I? Again and again, like a mantra. I know your body, your narrow, hairless chest, your birthmarks, your throat, the direction your beard grows, the shape of your hip bones, your fingers, your hands, your elbows, the way your balls hang, your knees, your feet, the smell of your sweat, the taste of your mouth. I know it all in every detail.

"Em?"

"Why are you being so unkind?"

"I'm asking what's wrong with you. Is that unkind?"

"You ask it so ..."

"So how?"

"I don't know."

He clenches his fists. "I'm trying to understand something about you."

"Really?"

He looks at her, his teeth on his lower lip. Put your arms round me, she thinks. He sets his cup down. He digs screws and nails out of his trouser pocket, then starts sorting them on the draining board. She picks up her phone and Joseph's card from the table and slinks upstairs. She puts the potato knife that's still in her pocket on the windowsill. Then she takes two Valium out of the box and swallows them both together. She hangs her wet clothes over the radiator. She's got hiccoughs. Knowing a body so precisely—is that the same as knowing the interior of a person? Does one follow from the other? In that body and in the endless sum of reactions and cadences and the way everyday actions are carried out, is there a core? *Peer Gynt*. How did it go again? You can peel the onion, but you can go on peeling until there's nothing left because an onion has only skins, no core, no pip, no hidden diamond. She crawls under the soft quilt. If only Bruch would come and lie next to her, press his warm body against her while the rain seeps in through all the cracks in the house.

Chapter 16

WHEN HE'D FINISHED scrubbing the carpet, he came to sit next to her on the bed. He stroked her back. Before she'd formulated the thought in her head, he articulated it.

"I didn't clean the carpet first because I decided that was more important. I thought I'd leave you in peace for a bit. In case that's what you wanted. I thought you might want that." The cheek she'd slapped was redder than the other.

"Yes."

"I ..."

"Yes?"

"Er."

"I'm sorry."

"Me too."

"Bruch." Her short, powerless words floated across the room. He was trying to reassure her, but he was doing it in a secret language. He said she could depend on him. "Perhaps it was just that chicken."

"What? What chicken?"

"A kind of food poisoning." It just slipped out. They hadn't eaten chicken.

"That seems pretty unlikely."

"Oh."

"But it's possible. It's a possibility." He said it hurriedly. He knew she was lying.

"Yes."

"Shall I ..."

"What?"

"Can I do anything?"

"What?"

"Is there anything I can do for you?"

"Mm."

"Or shall I ..."

"What?"

"Shall I leave you in peace?"

"Yes."

"For a bit. I'll leave you for a bit. Then I'll come and see how you're doing."

He left the room briskly, in silence, and shut the door carefully, warily; she could imagine him doing it, slowly letting go of the door handle, his head to one side and his eyes cast down. Of course she thought about it. About the fact that her unexpected physical reflex meant it was not as harmless, settled, irrelevant as she'd imagined. Of course she played with the idea of telling him. But then she fell asleep. An hour later she was woken by Bruch bringing her tea and strawberries. They didn't mention the incident again. Emilia forgot it had taken place. Just as she forgot that the rape had taken place. She forgot about it because she was happy. She was happy because she'd forgotten about it. Or did she merely think she was happy? Could you call happiness based on eliminating crucial aspects of yourself happiness at all? Could you say that something on closer examination wasn't happiness even though it felt as though it was? Does happiness actually have anything to do with those things? Isn't happiness in its purest intangible form a long way away from … events? But she didn't forget it. The truth is that she never forgot and in certain periods she thought about it every day.

Downstairs she can hear Bruch hitting wood with his hammer. Out of the corner of her eye she spots the knife. From now on she'll carry a knife, and she won't be afraid to use it. This little potato knife is useless. She needs a knife with a blade that folds into the handle and is opened by a spring. What's that called? A clasp knife? She still hasn't been up to the attic. Is it completely finished now? Won't they be coming back? The cold grey midday light makes everything pale. She mustn't oversleep. Not again. She must go downstairs at half past two and pretend there's nothing wrong and drive off to fetch the boys. Is Bruch going back to work? Why is he home? Oh no, she can't fetch the boys. Not after the Valium. She'll have to go by bicycle. But cycling there takes more than half an hour. And she can't carry two children on the bike. She'll have to fetch Leo first and then Osip. But if she does that, Bruch will ask why. And if she says why, he'll fetch them himself. Unless he's gone. But if he's gone, she can't leave Leo at home alone. If he's gone, maybe she'll drive after all. It's only a short distance. And it's only on the way back, with the boys on board, that she really must make sure nothing goes wrong. Although. She does need to get there. A switchblade. That's what it's called. Bruch ought to bring her tea and strawberries again. It's not impossible that he's thinking back on that first quarrel too. If he does, if he brings me strawberries, I'll tell him everything. And if he doesn't—she says it out loud, her voice sounding strange—if he doesn't bring strawberries, I won't tell him anything. If, then; if, then.

When she wakes up it's dark. There's tea and a plate of biscuits on the bedside table. It's quarter to nine. It's still raining. The house is quiet. She puts her phone to charge and looks at incoming messages. Colleagues, clients, Bruch twenty times over, Leo's school. In the mirror she sees that she looks miserable. The children are asleep. She adjusts Leo's blanket and puts his monkey, which has fallen to the floor, into his arms. She washes her hair and stands under the shower for a long time. She feels better. Everything's fine again. Or reasonably so. She needs to go downstairs, apologize, say it's over, her mood, which she doesn't understand herself. Will Bruch accept that? She can convince him, by behaving entirely normally. By being alert and clearheaded. By asking questions, not forgetting. She'll help with his flood defences, examine the measures to be taken. And she must write a letter of resignation. Then she won't need to think about that any longer. Then she can devote all her energy and all her time to their life together. Then everything really will go better and this episode will have an ending. It will have started and finished. That would be good. It's possible. It's happened before. There is no time and no opportunity to be alone. But it's possible. She gets dressed. She puts on a little makeup. She looks fine now.

Music is playing. Bruch is sitting at the table. His laptop is open and there are sheets of paper. On the floor are crates with things in them. In a quick glance she makes out food, string, a radio, matches. They're not going to evacuate. They're going to move up into the attic. She thinks of photos from the 1953 floods, of church spires sticking out of the water, people climbing into boats from attic windows. Bruch is sitting with his strong narrow back to her. His hair is getting long.

"Hello."

"Hello." He doesn't turn round.

"Sorry, I don't know what was wrong with me, food poisoning, nervous breakdown. At any rate. It's over." Food poisoning. There she goes again, she ought to say chicken and see what he does.

"Really?"

"Yes." She goes to sit at the table opposite him. "Really. Update me." She points at the tabletop.

"I've rung Jacob."

"What? Why?"

"I didn't believe you were with him."

"Jesus."

"But even if you weren't with him, he'd probably have told me you were. He confirmed your story, but still, what's that worth?"

"What's that worth?"

"At night you're not in bed. You're exhausted. You're remote and withdrawn."

"I slept really badly."

"Yes. But why?"

"Why?"

"Why."

"Can we talk about it later?"

"We can do anything, Emilia."

"Then we'll talk about it later, okay? I need a bit of time to recover."

"You going out?"

"Huh?"

"You look as if you're going out." He thinks she's having an affair! Maybe she should let him have that delusion. Maybe it's the only way to get beyond this.

"Tell me about the water. I'm behind."

Bruch stands up and takes a pointless turn around the kitchen. He stops at the table then takes the same turn again. Who's the one who is acting strangely?

"Bruch."

"No."

No. Emilia feels like a child made to sit in the corridor. She has to overcome that feeling. She has to do something. She's the guilty one.

"You hungry?" he asks. Too late. She nods and he starts putting cheese and butter and tomatoes and bread on the table. It might be more accurate to say flinging rather than putting, but perhaps she can't tell the precise difference between the two at the moment either.

"When we'd just moved here, those first few weeks, that late summer, Leo in his reed basket. Can you remember? Neither of us was working. Do you still remember? Remember how happy we were?" It's just like in that bar where they sat after the performance, when she reminded him about the pregnancy test. He looks as if she's trying to lure him into something. "I don't mean anything by it, it's just that I remembered."

"What do you mean you don't mean anything by it?"

"What I say."

"That's something you say when you do mean something by it. When you mean something else. What do you really mean? Are you taking stock of our marriage?"

"No, I'm not! Shut up!" They sit across from each other in silence. Then he picks up the knife and starts to cut bread. He spreads butter on it and slices the cheese. He pours tea for her. He explains the situation. He has nailed plates to the bottoms of the doors and piled sandbags the full length of the house.

"How did you manage all that, actually?" Sand is heavy. She's seen how much effort and time those last bags cost him and how little space they took up.

"Robert and his boys helped me."

"Who's Robert?"

"That odd-job man. The stairs have been postponed."

"What?" Jesus, she's been completely oblivious. Did she know he was called Robert? What else has she missed? Bruch is still talking. He's bought a pump for the cellar and he'll put emergency supplies in the attic. It's still raining and the water level is expected to rise further. The children could stay with Douwe and Sophie. Then Leo can go to school as normal. Bruch has taken some of the holiday owed to him. Excitement is now creeping into his account. He doesn't want to evacuate, not because he's unwilling to abandon the house to its fate or because he doesn't recognize the authority of the council bureaucrats but because he's enjoying this. She asks whether he's seen the wet patches in the conservatory. He shrugs. With the pump in the cellar that'll soon be resolved. They drink tea and eat bread and cheese. He puts his hands on her hands. She says she thinks the kitchen looks great.

When they get up and clear the table and turn off the light, he puts his arms around her and pulls her to him. He smells of sweat. He strokes her back, then rests his hands on her buttocks. Her breathing falters and she tries to think of a way out of his grasp. The lights are already off, she's already been upstairs, she can't suddenly refuse to go upstairs again. He pokes his fingers under the waistband of her trousers, lifts her jumper with his other hand, pinches her side and softly draws circles on her skin with his fingernails. She leans limply against him, a dizzying silence in her head. He whispers her name. She needs to say something too. And to do something. She can't move her arms. He hooks his fingers into her hair. She thinks of those strawberries again. How could she have been capable of it then and not now? Thank god she took that Valium, otherwise she'd be in a complete panic by this point. He lets go of her, takes her other hand, and leads her with him. They go upstairs, slowly, her eyes level with his hips. She still has a few metres, still a few minutes. They undress in the dark. It's cold in the room. Outside the window the darkness is complete. They slide under the covers. He kisses her throat, lays his head on her chest. She still can't move. She thinks of Eddy, and Marieke who froze as she underwent his touch. They didn't deal with him firmly enough. Eddy. Bastard.

"Emilia?" He lifts his head, floats above her face; she knows it's him. She needs to throw up. She needs to make herself as soft and immobile and accessible as possible.

The door opens.

"Dad? I had a bad dream."

Leo.

Everyone sleeps in their own bed, is what they've agreed, but she takes him in between them. His flannel pyjamas against her skin, his soft hair under the palm of her hand. In his neck she finds Bruch's hand and lays her own on top. A line meanders from here to the past, a line through time. The moment attaches itself without any difficulty to the start, to the start of their life together, to the start of Leo's life, when happiness was an intoxicated state of being and not something that could be unmasked. Time is a curve; years ago is closer now than yesterday.

Chapter 17

WHEN SHE GETS home he's standing at the window with his back to her. She hangs her coat on the door handle and kicks her rubber boots into the hallway. In the playground nobody was talking about anything but the water. Several children weren't in school because their parents had decided to leave the village. From under the floor comes the monotonous sound of the pump. She's tired. She couldn't sleep last night. She'd been in bed half the day. At first it was good to have Bruch and Leo so close to her, but then she started to feel hot and short of breath and trapped by their warm limbs on top of hers. She wriggled her hand out from under Bruch's hand, lifted Leo's arm away, and silently slipped out of bed. She crept out of the room the way she used to creep out of the house as a child, one foot in front of the other, sometimes waiting for several minutes to make sure nobody had heard her, that everything was still the way it was. She was afraid of Bruch, afraid he'd wake as soon as she got up and come after her to finish what they'd started. She crept downstairs and went to the conservatory. There she opened her laptop and sat wrapped in a blanket on the sofa. Was she imagining it, or was the sofa damp? She finally read Marieke's email, the reactions of all the staff, the mails from Josepha, the mails from Eddy to her and Josepha. In one of Eddy's, sent only to her, he wrote how disappointed he was in her friendship. She stared at that sentence for a while.

She started to write a letter of resignation but realized she couldn't simply give up her job, because she was part-owner. They would have to reach an agreement, financially; she had no idea how. In a mail to Josepha and Eddy she wrote that she wanted to come to an arrangement with them about her departure, and that the situation now, with Eddy, wasn't the reason, just the final drop in the bucket. In what bucket, she wondered, and she scrapped the sentence. Then she deleted the whole email. With some people it becomes apparent only when they get to a certain age just how annoying they are, as if youth smoothed the edges of their shabby characters. Eddy was such a person. She realized now that he'd always been a prick. But they were four, and somehow or other Eddy devolved his swagger onto the rest of them, who had less of it, and spread out over the group like that it was diluted. But as an individual, and on further examination, Eddy had always been a prick and Josepha was too soft. Was she taking stock? Perhaps Bruch had been right when he said that. But it wasn't about their marriage—where did he get that idea? She was standing with her arms outstretched on the other side of the Mississippi, trying to reach him ... She ought to go back upstairs, lift Leo out of their bed and gently lay him in his own bed and then lie down next to Bruch, touch him, wake him.

She looked on the internet for information about

flooding and found the site Bruch had consulted—
or at least it mentioned all the steps he'd taken and
had them summed up point by point. After a few
hours she went back. She lay as close to the edge of
the bed as possible and read a book by torchlight.
Eventually she fell asleep.

A series of daily duties pushed the morning on-
wards. Making sandwiches, chivvying the children,
who'd have liked nothing better than to hang out in
their pyjamas with their toys but needed to eat,
dress, and brush their teeth. Leo was weepy and
said he had a stomachache.

He was once stung by a wasp. Emilia thought he
was faking, jealous of Osip who'd been stung earlier
in the day and got lots of attention, so she waved it
off. Then she saw the expanding lump on his leg.
How could he have been so unconvincing when he
screamed? How could she have missed the pain in
his reaction so completely? This morning she laid
her hands on Leo's warm tummy and asked where it
hurt. She held him tight and comforted him and
promised to tell the teacher, saying they'd come and
fetch him if it didn't get better. That was enough for
the time being. She thought: I'll take you there, I'll
stash you away, because you're better off with your
class, because I don't know how I'm going to get
through the day, because I don't trust myself. When
she looked up, she caught Bruch giving her such a
cool, distant look it terrified her.

On the way home she drove more and more slowly.

Bruch turns round.

"So?" he says.

Bursting through her resolve to be open and pleasant, irritation flares in her. What's this *so*? She waits. He does nothing.

"Just give me a task. Tell me what I have to do." She says it as cheerfully as possible.

"Maybe you'd like to pack a bag for the children. This afternoon I'm taking them to Sophie. By tomorrow we won't have a garden any longer, our house will be right at the edge of the river."

"Do the boys know?"

"We can take them there together."

"Okay."

"Don't you have to work?"

"No."

"Oh."

"I'm leaving. But I don't know what position that puts me in. Financially. I don't know what my involvement is. I'll have to investigate."

"And what are you going to do then?"

"Oh, you know."

"Do I?"

"I take it I can coast for a while."

"And then?"

"I'll just keep writing and doing research."

"There's probably a competition clause."

"I'll see. I don't want to squeeze them for all I can get."

"Precisely."

"I don't believe in it anymore."

"In what?"

"The sos, Eddy and Josepha."

"Fallen out of love?"

"Yes, something like that."

There's a pause.

"With the SOS."

"Yes, that's what we were talking about."

"Not with you."

"Why do you say that?"

"Because that's what you're thinking."

"Am I?"

She should go over to him and put her arms around him. She should lean her head against him. She should hit him. She should bang her head against him. Standing there like that, he looks as lost as she feels.

"Don't you think it's ..." He searches for a word, finds it, rejects it, then uses it after all, stretching it out, "... *strange* that you didn't consult me first? It's part of our lives, isn't it?" He's pressing his toes to the floor, she notices, he's pushing himself away, his foot is pushing itself away.

"What?"

"Time, money ... consequences. For god's sake, Emilia."

"It's my decision." She's hungry. They haven't eaten yet; behind his back lie the ruins of breakfast.

"Of course."

"My business, my money, my decision. You could hardly refuse to let me, so ..." She walks to the kitchen counter, fishes a slice of bread out of the bag, looks for the peanut butter.

"That's not the point."

"Why do I have to consult you about everything if consultation couldn't possibly lead to a different outcome."

"Because we share our lives with each other!"

"But if your opinion isn't relevant ... not to the decision ... then it surely doesn't matter if ..."

"You seriously mean that, don't you?"

But Emilia doesn't mean anything, or at any rate she doesn't think she does. It seems she's just saying whatever comes to mind, as if she believes every thought that arises. He's shaking his head, so emphatically, so illustratively, like a bad actor. She spreads peanut butter on her bread, then takes a bite. She turns round.

"I'm just saying stuff. I don't know what I think." She's talking with her mouth full. Has he always done that, clench his fists? He's started doing it the last few weeks. It's only a matter of time before he punches her. Otherwise why are they standing up, anticipating something he probably isn't anywhere near realizing with his brain, perpetually at the ready? Those fists. That foot.

"Will you be careful?"

"What?"

"With that aggression?"

"What are you talking about?"

See, he still has no idea. He presses his right fist into his left palm. She points at it. He sees it too, and then slowly, despondently, he shakes his head. Bruch walks away, leaving her behind in the kitchen. A blue plastic bucket is floating across the garden. She needs to pack bags for the boys.

He hit her in the face with his fist, he kicked her, he planted his forearm across her throat, he twisted her arms behind her back, he squeezed her throat with both hands. He called her names.

Bruch comes back into the kitchen and starts clothing each of the table legs in a bin bag, then taping them at the top. He lifts the chairs onto the table. He says nothing to her.

He pulled the cover off the pillow and stuffed her head into it. He pulled her trousers down and away. She heard him spit.

Bruch has finished with the table. What will he do next? She didn't consult him about leaving the sos, but he doesn't consult her either. He simply tells her that the children are going to stay with Douwe and Sophie. And what are *they* going to do?

"Would you help me with the sofa first? I want to put it in the bedroom for now." She follows him into the conservatory. It's a green-and-grey-striped sofa with slightly curved legs. They toss the cushions and the blanket onto a chair, then each take one end and carry the thing to the stairs.

"At the turn we'll tilt the legs that way." He indicates the direction with a toss of his head. "Do you want to be at the top or the bottom? I think it's best if you're at the top."

"Then I'll go up."

When it gets stuck at the turn they rest for a moment. The sofa is heavy and awkward. Upstairs her phone rings. She listens to it until it stops. Then they manoeuvre the sofa into a more upright position. He pushes, she pulls, it starts to move and they get it onto the landing. The door to the bedroom is too narrow, so they tilt the sofa onto its back, tip the whole thing vertical, steer the legs around the doorframe, wrench and push and get it inside. They place it against the foot of the bed and Bruch sits on it. He's had the sofa longer than he's had her; it's rather scruffy, it needs reupholstering. Her telephone rings again. It's Jacob.

"Emilia here."

"Little one. Is Bruch sitting next to you?"

"How do you know that?"

"I can tell from your voice. Everything okay?"

"Hmmm ..."

"Shall I call you later?"

"Yes. Better."

"You ring me."

"Sure. Bye." She hangs up and waves the phone in Bruch's direction. "Jacob."

"Short conversation."

"I'll go and pack those bags." She closes the door behind her.

The way some people suddenly become Catholics, could you suddenly one day say that you don't want sex anymore, not ever again? He goes downstairs. She can hear the anger in his footsteps. She throws soft toys, pyjamas, clothes, and toothbrushes into a bag. She strips the beds and stuffs the sheets into the washing machine. She tosses scattered toys into boxes and drawers. She arranges the loose stones and shells and trinkets on Leo's windowsill. She organizes Osip's cuddly toys into a group portrait. She doesn't want a celibate life. She only wants to say that to get the idea out of the way. Just as she wants to let him keep the illusion of an affair.

She could leave him, too.

Chapter 18

IT WAS EARLY summer, late afternoon, and Emilia had just been presented with her degree certificate. Her brothers had guzzled the wine at the reception without even taking off their coats. She'd gone into town with them afterwards and they'd had Chinese on Hoogstraat. Jacob chewed with his eyes shut. He drank four pots of Jasmine tea. The heroin episode was still fairly fresh and Jacob had been back only a few weeks from his stay in a clinic. His greed seemed to have increased in every other direction. When she looked at his face with those closed eyes, at that image of concentrated abandonment, she felt something radical slumbering within her, the readiness to do something crazy. The hair above his eyebrows was too short and cut too straight. Viktor had started on one of his tiresome tirades against capitalism. Emilia rolled roasted duck into pieces of pancake and nibbled at cucumber julienne. She was supposed to go to a party afterwards. Eddy, Martyn, and Josepha had been presented with their degrees too, and they'd hired a room above a bar. She had gifts and the text of her speech for Jos in her bag. But after they dropped Viktor at his house, she continued hanging around on the Nieuwmarkt with Jacob.

If she could choose a moment to fix and experience again, just briefly, before time drove her on down the track, it would be that evening. She'd graduated without her father and mother; she'd become something, a sociologist, an adult; she'd broken free from her childhood for good. And she wasn't yet tied to anything else. If you care about someone—a man, a child—you irrevocably lose something of yourself, but you ignore the fact because what's lost is worth little. You lose your lack of a definitive form. Now she'd love to be so ... free. To go back to the moment before her life was settled.

"Emilia!!" She pulls herself away from her thoughts, away from the window. She tugs open the door to Leo's room. Bruch is standing there. He no longer looks like her husband, a doctor. He looks like a bulldozer driver, a deckhand, a manual labourer. His face is dirty. There's a sticking plaster on his thumb. Her raincoat hangs from his outstretched arm.

"We're going." He scans the tidied room. What is he thinking? They're removing the children. They're piling up the furniture. They're nailing the doors shut. They're closing themselves in.

She walks behind him up onto the dike to his car.

"Why are they going to Sophie and Douwe's and not to Amsterdam?" she calls out to his back.

He slows his pace but doesn't turn round. He gets in. She gets in. He starts the engine and puts his hands on the wheel.

"I don't think you can drop a toddler and an infant with Jacob and Lieke."

"No?"

"For a start, they're never home."

"Oh, right."

"You'd have to go with them."

"Hmm."

"Wouldn't you?"

"And you don't want that?"

"I don't want to do this whole thing alone." He stresses *whole*.

"So it's not so much that you want me to be here, it's just that you don't want to do everything on your own."

"I'd like us to do this together."

"Okay."

"Okay?"

"Yes, of course."

"Good."

"Good."

Can such a dismal bunch of words bring two people together? They're married, they have a history, they have children—all things that mean this won't go wrong. It's not something to be taken lightly, she hears her Aunt Jane say in a suddenly crystal-clear memory. She, her mother and aunt at the kitchen table in the dusty late afternoon light at the back of the house; outside, the sky and the meadows, always wind, a rotary washing line bearing faded clothes, slowly turning, squeaking. Uncle Piet moves in with his girlfriend. Her mother says levity is the enemy of a marriage.

They fetch Osip first. They exchange a few comments with the staff of the crèche about the weather and the water. In the school playground the same conversation is repeated. Bruch knows everybody, far better than she does. He knows their names. People enjoy talking with him. She looks at his getup. He's updating them on the house. Someone asks about the pump. Someone else asks about the sand. He lays his hand on an arm as he replies. Water levels are mentioned. Millimetres. Bruch asks questions in return. Other people too are experiencing flooding, but Emilia and Bruch are the only ones who live outside the dike. Emilia stands next to her husband and says nothing, gripping her umbrella and plucking at Osip's hair. Schooltime ends. The teachers come out one by one, each with a string of children behind them like good little ducklings. Leo runs towards his family in high spirits, pleasantly surprised to see all three of them there, but he slows up halfway, for precisely the same reason. Foreboding. She snuggles him, awkwardly keeping the umbrella up. When she tells him that he and Osip are going to stay with friends his face darkens. In the car he starts to cry. Bruch ignores it. Emilia is flung back and forth between empathy and irritation.

"See it as an adventure," she says. "It's only for a couple of nights."

"I want to be with you."

"Mum and Dad need to work very hard; we have a lot of things to do."

"But I can help, can't I?"

"No, treasure, you can't."

His crying gets louder.

"I think it's good," says Osip. Leo gives him a thump. Now Osip starts crying too. Emilia rummages in the glove compartment.

"What are you looking for?"

"Sweets." There are all kinds of things in there, but no sweets. She unfastens her seatbelt, gets up onto her knees on the seat, and pulls off the head-rest. Leo looks angry. Osip pouts. Emilia squeezes a hand, strokes a head, hums a little, promises it will be fun.

"Have they got children?"

"Big children."

"Can I go to school tomorrow?"

"Tomorrow you can, but after that it's the week-end."

"Do I have to stay there all weekend?"

"Maybe."

"Don't want to!" He starts crying again. Emilia asks Bruch in English whether they shouldn't just take them home. It surely won't … not all at once … not upstairs …

Bruch just grunts a little.

"What are you saying?" Leo shouts.

"Come on, Emilia!" Bruch throws her a glance.

"What?"

"Don't be such an idiot."

"Okay."

"Why are you talking English?"

"Just because."

"Because I'm not allowed to hear."

"Yes."

"You're stupid."

"You're sweet."

He hits her hand when she reaches out to stroke his head.

"Mum, you're sweet too," shouts Osip. Bruch turns onto the drive of the house next to the house where

Douwe grew up. Or was it Sophie? On the door is a sign saying *Welcome*. Leo reads it, his finger moving from one letter to the next.

"Maybe it's there specially for you."

"Really?"

Sophie's approach dissipates any remains of rebellion against the forced sleepover. Emilia immediately detects in her an ability to make children happy without spoiling them. A thoroughly reliable person. At the bar that separates the kitchen from the dining room, they drink a perfect espresso. Emilia tries to shake off her aversion to spotlessness. Leo has discovered paper and crayons discreetly laid ready for them, and he's now drawing a boat with everyone in it. Osip stands next to him, looking in admiration at what his big brother is doing. Emilia presses her nose into Leo's warm little neck and whispers "see you soon" in his ear. Osip gives her a few wet kisses then pushes her away.

As if they're already wading through water, they slowly struggle back to the car together. They drive home in silence and leave the car in the verge by the dike. Their house is sticking up out of the water not like a rock but like a piece of forgotten wreckage. It's not raining. A heavy grey murky sky lowers over them. There's nothing around that could be reflected in the grimy surface of the water. No animals to be seen. A few metres behind Bruch, she walks down from the dike to the front door. The hallway is dry but there's water on the kitchen floor. The pump that was churning away in the cellar is now standing in the middle of the kitchen. Emilia doesn't understand how a pump like that could do any good. Water in the kitchen means the water level has reached their floor, and changing anything there, locally, on the eighty square metres covered by their house, seems impossible to her. The sand, the wood—it's all a lost cause; the water has demolished the boundary. Bruch turns on the radio and consults his phone for water levels and weather forecasts. In the Ardennes and Northern France the rivers have swollen even further in the rain. He uses a marker pen and the tape measure to turn the doorframe into a ruler. He notes the water level on a piece of paper he then puts in his trouser pocket.

"Everything has to go up."

In the hours that follow they carry everything upstairs: tables, chairs, bags, boxes. Emilia keeps filling a crate and a large rucksack with books and lugging them up to Osip's room, where she unpacks before repeating the process. Bruch unscrews the doors of the lower cupboards in the kitchen. With a persuasiveness clearly aimed at himself, he explains that kitchens are made of materials that can withstand water. But she looks at the skirting at the base, at the thin veneer inside the cupboards: somewhere between wood and cardboard. The clouds have come right down to hang in misty plumes over the land, trapping the light. The water is already more than a centimetre higher than it was just now. If the house collapses, if the damage is irreparable, if they have to move to a different house without being able to pay off the mortgage, if they're left with no choice but to live in a tiny two-room apartment, somewhere around here because in the city even that's too expensive, if she therefore tries to squeeze everything she can out of the sos, or, worse, for the sake of financial security has to go on working there, if they're living in two rooms, where they have to turn a sofa into a bed at night, if nothing is left of their life in its present form, with space, distance, freedom, luxury ... if the river is no longer nearby, if she hates it for what it's taken from them, if, in accordance with Dutch tradition, they lose everything they own to the water ... if they're left with nothing but each other ...

"We're done," Bruch barks. "We're going upstairs."

Chapter 19

THEY BOUGHT A van, built a bed into it, and travelled around Italy. Down the Adriatic coast, round the heel, sole, and tip of the boot, and up alongside the Mediterranean. At night they parked as close to the sea as possible and in the mornings they swam themselves awake. In a shabby-looking restaurant in a deserted holiday village, where they ate fabulous squid, Bruch asked her to marry him. She said no. She didn't believe in it, in a contract with a third party, the state or the government, in something so outmoded and unnecessary.

Bruch, an intelligent man, susceptible to a well-reasoned argument, not particularly traditional by nature, couldn't understand it at all. Unnecessary rebellion, he thought. Rationalist hubris. He gazed at the sea, narrowed his eyes, looked like a sailor. The sky was blue; the wind was gentle but with something exuberant about it. A girl in a chequered dress brought them a fresh carafe of wine. Bruch ate bread. She couldn't gauge how disappointed he was. Making love to you, she thought, means forgetting everything, daring to jump, daring to sink. If nothing's at stake, then everything's just a game. She realized that her objection was a leftover from her previous life, from before Bruch, before her attacker, before the few small steps that had finally taken her away from Jacob. Her no was an embrace of a kind of autonomy from which she no longer expected anything. So then she said yes. But she said it too softly and it coincided with the sharp sound of a chair leg sliding across the tiles as Bruch got up to take a piss.

He put his hand on her hair, then brought it down past her ear and her neck and into her blouse. She sighed. He leaned over towards her, said "you're sighing" and walked away, one loose sole making a flapping noise on the paving. He hadn't heard! She looked for a pen but didn't have one. Then she decided to use her finger to write YES in the sauce on his plate, but there was no sauce left on his plate. The sea was calm and looked shallow, as if it was just a few inches of water covering an endless plain.

Another day went by before she managed to make her yes audible. They were lying in the van.

"About your question."

"Yes?"

"Whether I'll marry you."

"Yes?"

"I just wanted to ... er ... come back to it."

"Yes?"

"Yes."

"Really?"

"Yes."

He looked horribly satisfied, as if everything was going precisely as he expected. She wanted to take it back, but he pulled her to him, hugged her and whispered things in her ear. The world opened up in a new dimension. She had committed herself. She thought about how her brothers would react, then cast the image away. And she thought: we can do whatever we choose, there's nobody we need to ask; we can marry, have children, never go back to the Netherlands.

"Is there anything else I should know?" He was lying on top of her and she asked what he meant by that. Did you have to exchange sexual résumés after saying yes, or something? Was that part of the ritual? He said it wasn't. He said it was a joke. At that moment she was so wrapped up in her own secrets that it didn't occur to her he might have one of his own, a secret that consumed him, that made his heart palpitate when he thought about telling her.

It's a romantic memory, the van, the trip, the proposal, and her response. The truth is that she was tired, and still afraid. She accepted marriage as a promise of a new beginning in life, of leaving other things behind for ever, other loves, wounds incurred. Nothing could be better or more definitive. It was a flight, it was seeking refuge in the shelter of the bell curve.

Chapter 20

"JESUS, BRUCH, HAVEN'T we got any wine?"

On the table is a bottle of water with two glasses. Before coming up he turned the power off at the mains. The room, lit by a few candles and a gas lamp, smells of wood and sounds hollow.

"We need to keep our heads clear."

"I'm not talking about a cask, love, just a glass."

"Somewhere in one of those." He points to the wall of boxes and crates. That gesture, his choice of words, his tone, his disapproving look—they all feed her recalcitrance. She starts lifting the boxes off the stack and opening them until she finds a bottle of wine. Screw-top, thank god. She sees him watching.

"You too?"

Without saying anything he slides his glass towards her. He points to a clock.

"I've set the alarm. We'll go downstairs every two hours to see how high the water has risen. We'll make a note, with the time."

"And if we're asleep?"

"Then the alarm will wake us."

"Okay."

"That's what I just said, didn't I?"

"Yes, sorry, good, fine. Set it then, the alarm."

"I already have."

"Of course. Cheers."

"Yes." Then after a pause: "Cheers." It takes him an effort to say it.

She drains her glass in one go.

"Do you think I'm cheating on you?"

He's silent for such a long time that she starts to wonder whether she's actually asked the question.

"No. I don't think that."

"I thought you did."

"Well, I don't."

"What did you think, then?"

"What do you mean by that?"

"What did you think was going on?"

"Was?"

"Or is."

"Why don't you just tell me what's the matter, instead of leaving me to speculate?"

We must make a baby, she thinks. It's perfectly possible. Statistics about the fertility of mothers aged over forty are almost all derived from eighteenth-century data about French church congregations. A new child is a new beginning. And a good story. *You were conceived during the great flood. In the attic. Just before the river swallowed the house. Your parents were swimming in the garden while the seed swam in your mother. They were tired, reconciled, your parents; they were aware something new had begun. A little later the seed entered the egg, then came the implantation and the endless division of cells, the rampant growth that completed and fulfilled itself in you. Which explains why you love swimming!* In her mind she sees a little girl who looks just like she herself did when she was small, and behind her stand her two brothers, exactly the same as hers, almost exactly the same portrait. Except that nobody dies. And nobody succumbs to regret. She refills her glass.

"I had a conversation with a few of the parents in the playground about one-in-a-hundred chances. They thought it would be worth looking up when it last flooded here. So I told them the joke about the operation that has only a ten percent chance of success. Do you know that one?"

"No."

"A patient is wheeled into the operating theatre, terrified because of his minimal chances of survival. The surgeon says, don't worry sir, nine have already died under my hands today."

"Did they think that was funny?"

"Yes, I think so. They laughed. A little."

Bruch has stretched out on one of the beds with a book on his chest. A baby. To feel that absolute boundlessness again. The misty boundary between one body and another, the vanishing point of a purely physical existence. An intensity for which no good word exists. Love, but in a specific form.

"Are you trying to tell me something?" Bruch asked.

"No. Nothing."

Her eyes sting and her head is throbbing. She holds her hands flat to the cold floor. If only the alarm would go off. When the alarm sounds, Bruch will go downstairs and when he's down there the fog in her head will have a chance to lift. When he comes back up, they'll have exactly two hours to clear the barriers out of the way and make a baby. Bounded by the next time the alarm sounds, accompanied by a hundred and twenty times sixty times two ticks of the clock. Fourteen thousand four hundred dry and reassuring beats of time. She can count them if she can't find any other way to concentrate. Two hours, and within those hours a clear task. What are two hours of your life? When she counts the days since her last period it's precisely right. Might her desire have been prompted by her physical receptivity? Yesterday she didn't know she wanted another child. Today all she doesn't yet know is how to bridge the half metre between her and Bruch. He's a stranger, a man with a book on a bed, locked tight like a safe. Touch him, she tells herself. She's no longer afraid, but there is something preposterous about it.

"When I was in Amsterdam I ran into Vincent," she says.

"I know."

"How do you know?"

"He rang me that evening."

"He's not doing too well."

"No, that was obvious."

"Why didn't you tell me he said he'd seen me?"

"Why didn't you tell me you'd seen him?"

"Forgot. He feels old."

"Yes."

"It was rather ... pathetic."

"It felt as if death was stalking him."

"He's in his mid-fifties."

"Something like that."

"What are you reading?"

"*Notes from Underground*. A patient gave it to me."

She goes over and lies down next to Bruch and feels the heat of his body. He reads; time goes by. She thinks: things are improving by the minute with me and with us. A message comes in from Sophie with a picture of two sleeping boys. The alarm rings and Bruch goes downstairs. She fills her glass. What a crazy idea it had been to tell him after all this time; it would throw everything out of balance and take a huge amount of effort to get it all on an even keel again. For a while she'd been mesmerized by the conviction that there was a need to clear the air. But it's a strange modern idea that you can truly feel like yourself only under a cloudless sky. Life is full of debris and blemishes, full of cracks in the varnish. The notion that honesty is so important, more important than anything else, that you need to merge with your partner, that you ought to share your whole history, your whole reservoir of feelings, that it's a mistake, a missed opportunity or a form of indecency not to tell the person you love what has touched you in the past, that you should abandon the story of your life in order to end up together in the same, shared story ... Once and for all, she thinks: no. There's no inevitable connection between the facts and the truth. Candour and intimacy aren't extensions of one another. What a mad idea that she and Bruch were standing on opposite sides of a wide river. What a mad idea that because of her silence they couldn't now be deeply connected. What's wrong is not that she never told him about it; what's wrong is that it ever happened. But you can't do anything about that. And you don't need to bring past events out into the light in order to find consolation. They're together; she's safe; everything needs to be the way things are.

Bruch comes back and turns on the radio. The water in the kitchen has risen several more centimetres and it's now in the hall near the front door. It's started raining again, too. Clattering against the skylight. The local radio station is reporting on the evacuation of a village not far away. It's only a matter of time before they're forced to leave the house.

"You look feverish. Are you all right?"

"I'm going to write a book."

"Really?"

"A biography."

"Of who? Quetelet?"

"Of the average. I'm going to write a biography of the average." He looks at her and narrows his eyes. His head turns slightly to the left. Interest. "The history of the arithmetical average and the mean and the median. But also about how the average determines the norm, how we discern what's normal by recording what's most common. It's about being normal, belonging to the largest group, about who defines that group, about the implications of the exceptional. It's about the normal distribution as a construct. It's about outliers, do you know what they are?"

"Yes. What are they again?"

"Values that deviate significantly are explained as outliers and deleted from a dataset before the statistical calculations are carried out. And that produces a different value for the average than if they were included. Outliers can result from measurement errors or from exceptional events that you choose not to take into account, but there's no unambiguous mathematical criterion for declaring one particular result an outlier. It's a matter of interpretation, of subjective judgement. Statistics Netherlands calls it 'control and correction.' Some of the staff there do nothing but look at the statistics that come in to see if they can find any deviant data that need to be filtered out. They even look at the past, with the idea that the value of a particular statistic for this year shouldn't be radically different from its value for last year."

"You ought to get your hands on those outliers from Statistics Netherlands. Like the way Stella makes art out of waste, you could construct something out of all those rejected deviations." Stella is a friend of Bruch's. He once bought a small sculpture of hers made of steel and rubber that depicts a couple dancing; it's on his desk. It has always given Emilia an uncomfortable feeling.

"... about the average as an exception, for example when it's composed of extremes ..." While rattling on she's gone to sit astride him and she's put her hands under his jumper and his shirt, on the warm skin of his chest. The alarm clock is ticking.

"The average person."

"Quetelet had thoroughly practical concerns: which month people most often died or were born in, left-handedness, illness, height, weight, how many children."

"When was this again? You're blazing hot."

"1830. Your hands are cold." She leans forward and kisses his neck.

"Your face is red-hot, Emilia."

"But I feel good."

"Do you really?"

"You smell nice." She presses her face into his armpit.

He puts his hands under her clothes. It's true, she has a fever, her heart is throbbing at her temples. The water drumming above their heads is precisely like the sound of the rain then, twelve years ago, in his flat. He saved her. She'd been trying to think up ways to escape her life, to leave the Netherlands, to disappear from her family. She couldn't find her niche, there was no form of adult life she could reconcile herself to. She'd never fallen in love, she was too tied to Jacob. She'd had a relationship with a married former teacher of hers; they messed about a little, nothing in public, nowhere with any prospects. And then there was Bruch. He'd enticed her away from the extremities, he'd hauled love out of a clandestine corner and offered her the prospect of a life, together. He'd tempted her under the bell curve, right into the middle of the normal distribution. Suddenly she sees it all clear as day. Don't tell, she thinks, never tell. That bubble of cruelty and pain and humiliation must never be punctured and allowed to seep into the rest of her life.

She pulls his trousers down. Then she stands up and takes off her clothes. He lies there and looks at her. This is my body, she thinks, and this is my husband. She goes to sit on top of him again. The alarm clock ticks, the water rises; if you were a bird you'd see a house with flickering candlelight at its small attic window, standing in the middle of a raging river.

Chapter 21

HIS LIPS ARE moving. He's saying something. She tenses her muscles to draw him tightly inside her. Yes, she says as loudly as she can, me too! Maybe he said it's amazing or that he loves her, the things you say. His lips move again: Why aren't her ears working? Is she slowly being robbed of her senses? He stretches out his hand to her, towards her throat. Did she fight? Did she try to get free of his grip or to hurt him? Or did she need all her concentration to hold herself together, not fall apart, stay alive? There was a moment when she knew for certain that dying wasn't so terrible. What could be bad about total peace, a relaxation so deep and complete that you slowly disintegrate and disappear? No, she didn't fight. She lay as motionless as she could. In the beginning she spoke. She told him she wanted to talk to him and that afterwards he could do whatever he was planning to do but first she wanted them to talk. She still believed then in the rationality of argument, and in her own powers of persuasion. He didn't say anything in response, just put a hand over her mouth and when she again tried to speak he slammed his fist into her face and shouted.

Bruch turns her onto her back; he's above her now.

He, Bruch, not anyone else: kind, tolerant, loving. He says her name. His weight presses on her chest and it's hard to breathe. She tries to push him upwards a little, meanwhile moving her lower body to avoid any suggestion that she wants to stop. She puts her hands on her shoulders and sticks her elbows up in the air like peaks, so he can't get at her throat; it's all very simple, she just has to avoid that somehow, then she can shut it off. Above her pointed elbows she sees his face. He still has that undulating furrow over his eyes.

"Emilia!" Yes. That's me. "Emilia!" He pushes her arms apart and lays them above her head, defenceless. He keeps saying her name. He needs to finish this, she thinks. She mustn't lose sight of the goal. She tries to look sensual, opening her mouth. He lays his hands against the sides of her face. The sore throat she had after being throttled was just like the sore throat you get with flu. He puts the tips of his thumbs on the throbbing artery under the skin and she feels her heart in her throat, drumming against his thumbs. He increases the pressure slightly and then she lashes out. As if elastic has snapped in her limbs, elastic that has kept everything in shape until now. She hits him on the chin with her fist. Jesus, what on earth is she up to? That was completely the wrong reflex. Her legs kick out at him. Bruch tries to evade her but she makes contact with his knee. He yells and clutches it. She wants to stop but her body has different plans altogether. Bruch lets go of his knee, pulls her into his arms and holds her. She squirms and tries to bite him. He twists his head out of her reach and presses his arms around her.

"Sorry!" she screams. Why is she screaming? "I slipped!" She tries to free herself from his grasp.

"Hush Emilia, it doesn't matter, it doesn't matter."

"Bruch! Help!"

"I know I know I know I know." He hugs her tight, slowly squeezing the resistance out of her, and then sits up. Her teeth are chattering and her whole body is shaking. Her legs are no longer kicking, but the jolting still isn't under control. He piles blankets on top of her sweaty body and puts his hand to her forehead the way a doctor does. She's icy cold. She tries to wriggle out from under the covers. He stops her, with one hand.

"Calmly now. You have to calm down. I'm with you." Blood is pouring from his lip. He wipes his mouth and looks at the red streak on the back of his hand.

"I need to say something."

"You don't need to say anything, you need to stay lying down."

"I need to stay lying down."

"You don't need to say anything."

"I don't need to say anything."

"I already know, Emilia. I already know."

Did he come? She wasn't paying attention. She puts her hand between her legs in search of evidence. The fresh pine planks neatly aligned to the crest of the attic slowly start to billow. The sound of the rain is impossible to locate now. It's all around her and even inside her head. A yellow light flashes in the corner of her eye. She puts her hands on her abdomen. Bruch draws breath.

"You were wearing a green blouse with tiny white stars. Your arms stuck out of it to just past your elbows. The skin of your arms, sun-browned with blonde fuzz, your dark hair that fell lightly and softly past your throat onto your shoulders, your hands on the table, your short nails, your wrists that my hands could easily wrap around, your eyes, the freckles on your nose. You were so alive, so bubbly, so interested in me; when you smiled at me I floated free of the ground. I thought you were unbelievably pretty and funny. I couldn't get the smile off my face that whole evening and night. It took me all the effort I could muster to deal with my critically ill patients properly, not to insult them with my euphoria.

"When you didn't pick up the phone and in the days that followed, I knew something terrible had happened. That you were dead, run over, abducted, murdered. I was confident enough in myself not to think that you didn't want to see me anymore and confident enough in you to know that you wouldn't be so cowardly as to keep silent if that was how it was. I knew that the way you'd looked at me couldn't have changed completely unless something cataclysmic had happened. I rang you, left a message on your answerphone. After a few days I rang Jan, the friend who took me to that party, and asked him for your brother's number. Jacob was rude and unpleasant and refused to give me your address. After that I rang the sos. I got Eddy on the line. He said you were on holiday. I had to go to a conference in Maastricht, which gave me a distraction for a few days. The longer I spent not seeing you, the more my self-confidence deserted me. Without you around I only fell more intensely in love. I thought at my most cynical moment that it was a trick, a way to make me completely crazy about you. Then I tried to convince myself again that I'd dreamed you. That you'd been doing something else for ages already. On holiday. With someone. I thought I must be a total idiot. Worry gave way to self-pity. I went to bed with somebody. I tried not to think about you. I thought up stupid and ugly character traits for you. I tried to despise you.

"No one picked up your home phone and I couldn't leave any more messages. I was angry and wanted to tell you how I felt. The next Monday I rang the sos again. Eddy told me that somebody had beaten you up and you were in hospital. At first I thought he was joking, but he assured me it was true. You'd been attacked in your own home and battered. He said you had a broken jaw but apart from that nothing too serious and you were doing okay. I asked him which hospital you were in. He said you'd been in the Lucas. And he gave me your home address. He seemed to enjoy being able to tell me, knowing all this about you. I tried to imagine who would do a thing like that to you. I thought of Jacob, who'd been so abrupt with me, and of the party where I first saw you. When I left, you were lying on the floor between your two brothers. Jacob had his hand on your leg, an intimate, possessive gesture. I tried to remember whether you'd told me about any neighbours or flatmates, whether there were any nutcases in your vicinity. I realized I knew very little about you. Now and then I tried your phone again. One time the line was engaged. You never answered.

"After I'd managed to control myself for a few days, I rang a friend of mine who worked at the Lucas Andreas Hospital. I asked him to take a look in your file for me. He told me you'd been raped and he reeled off all the internal and external injuries, your broken jaw, broken fingers, broken ribs, the scratches and cuts; he told me your larynx had been so badly bruised by strangulation that you'd been unable to speak for several days. He'd copied the whole lot out. The file also said that apart from the police, you hadn't had any visitors.

"That evening I stood outside your door in the dark for at least two hours. I looked at your surname on the metal name plate, at the bubbled glass in the door, at the flaking paint, at the perfect gleaming roundness of your doorbell. I crossed the street and looked up at the windows. The only light showing was on the second floor. I saw no movement, no silhouettes, no shadows. The light eventually went out. I went home. I read somewhere that most rapes are committed by acquaintances, exes, dates, often by partners.

"I cycled or walked past your place every day, sometimes three times in a day. I hoped we'd see each other by chance. That seemed to me the only possibility left, luck, engineered by my hanging around in your street. It was too late now to ring your bell, to say I knew or to pretend not to know. After a while I stopped. It seemed logical to me, really, that you didn't have the appetite for a new love affair. I told myself that I'd lost you."

Bruch takes her hand. She lets him but doesn't squeeze back, just leaves her hand lying limply in his. She's no longer trembling; the cold of a moment ago has solidified and is holding her, pincer tight. Maybe this is more like what death is, not the warm disintegration of dissolving into the universe, not a heroin daze amplified, but this ice-cold petrification.

"I rang Mariette and spent a weekend with her. It was like old times and it felt miserable. I thought going back to something I'd already closed off would keep the way to you open somehow. Sure, I'd be messing about with someone else, but someone from the past, someone from before. I hadn't moved on. We planned to spend a few days in Brussels, just Mariette and me. I dreamed up kill-or-cure remedies to banish you from my thoughts and drive out my feelings of guilt.

"But then you rang. I spent the time between our phone conversation and your arrival at my house—what can it have been, no more than an hour—in a state of nervous excitement. First, I cancelled Mariette. I was hard and gruff because, no matter what, I had to prevent her from coming to my flat. I hung up while she was crying. It didn't affect me. I flung everything from my suitcase back into the wardrobe. I showered, changed, tidied up. It occurred to me that your body, so horribly violated, now healed, hadn't been touched by anyone since those events, that in a sense you were a virgin again, a ridiculous thought. I'm ashamed to say that the idea aroused me in spite of myself.

"When I opened the door you seemed so small, so fragile. I didn't know what to say. I hardly dared look at you. You immediately took off your shoes, which

I thought was odd. Was it a statement? You didn't seem like a victim. You were sovereign, ironic. And you were a complete stranger to me. Then you kissed me. I forced myself to do nothing at all except react, to do only what you invited me to do. I kept my eyes on you. I searched your face for signals to stop. I explored your body for scars. The ragged white line on your left thigh was of an earlier vintage, from childhood; I could tell by its edges that it had stretched as your skin grew. I assumed your jaw had been set and stitched from the inside. You had a mark on your belly that might have been transplanted skin. I'd never seen you naked before, I had nothing to compare. I looked at your throat and thought of that bruised larynx. Of your vocal cords, of the whisper in which you must have reported the crime and talked to your doctor. But I saw no stop signs, no barriers, no red light. You surrendered yourself. Afterwards your face was wet—with tears, I thought, but I hadn't seen you cry. I doubted myself. As if I'd been dreaming. Had I really been watching you closely? We lay side by side and looked at the ceiling. Exactly the way we're lying here now. I waited for you to tell me why you'd stayed away all those weeks. I waited for you to tell me why you were in my bed now.

"You said nothing. Even the next day. And then you went home.

"When you got home you rang me. As proof, you said, that the silence was over. But in the days that followed I realized the silence wasn't over at all. Why weren't you telling me anything? I gave it a week. I gave it another week. I gave it a month and then another. I forgot the deadline. I forgot the motive for telling you I knew. I understood that you didn't want it to come between us, at least that was how I interpreted the silence. I didn't manage to tell you that it was already there and that speaking about it would get it out of the way. I discussed it with Vincent. I know it's terrible for you to have to hear this, but he swore to me he'd never tell anyone and I think he's kept that promise. Anyhow, in those days he wasn't so, well, what you've described as pathetic. He was a good guy, with imagination and empathy, exactly what I needed. I chose to respect your preference for secrecy. He insisted it would set you free if I told you I knew. I was ashamed that I'd known for so long. He said it was perfectly possible to explain a thing like that. He said I should grab any chance I could to make it into something we shared ... Time and again there were opportunities, moments when I wanted to do exactly that: the first time I went to your flat and saw the place where it happened, when we went on holiday, when you came to live with me, when you threw up in the middle of a playful tussle, when we argued, when you seemed unreachable, when we got married, when you found out you were pregnant, when the midwife asked if you'd ever had an unpleasant sexual experience because you might relive it during labour and you said no. But it merged into the background. Life took over. I forgot about it. Or I chose to forget about it."

Emilia stares at a knot in the timber above her.

To horse! To sword! There are traitors abroad! a little

voice starts singing inside her, softly at first but gradually swelling to a roar.

Chapter 22

THE WATER THAT crept up the doorframe so calmly at first is now a swirling mass. It's no longer a puddle, a spillage, lying still and peaceful in the room, almost friendly. Now the river itself, its passage blocked by strange new obstacles such as walls, is pouring through the house and creating whirlpools under the stairs. Always from left to right, like a line of poetry, Bruch had said when it was still flowing safely between its banks. Emilia thinks of an anecdote about her grandpa driving his car into a canal. He struggled free and climbed out, then clutched his head and immediately dived back into the water, swam to his car, which had sunk to the bottom, found his hat, and came up again as the gentleman that he was. She sits halfway down the stairs. The debris of the shed comes swilling into the house through the window, with one beam crashing into the kitchen cupboards. Above the house is the whirr of a helicopter. She shivers in the grey morning light, her ears ringing.

They lay there, looking endlessly up at the attic ceiling. If we're quiet for as long as he spent talking, then time will turn back and the silence will erase everything he said, Emilia thought, and after a while she knew for certain: I was delirious; none of it happened.

Then he knelt down beside her again and looked at her.

"Say something," he begged. Not a dream.

"But you know everything already, don't you?"

"Emilia ..."

"You persuaded a doctor to breach his duty of confidentiality. You ferreted everything out, investigated everything, read all about it. You searched me for signs, inside and out. You've connected everything strange that I ever did to this and understood it in this context. You've reduced me, you've done exactly what I was trying to prevent. And I didn't know." She was shrieking now.

"That's not how it was!"

"I can only fill in and fill out a bit here and a bit there; you've drawn the picture already."

"No, no, no!"

"You made a case out of me. You've been thinking of me as a case all this time. You lived with it and tried to pretend that wouldn't matter."

"Not true!"

Locked up inside her, within a flaming shell of rage, something else is burning. A desire for consolation perhaps. Something she can't get at.

"No? What's left for me to tell you?"

"Who did it?"

"Don't you have any friends who work for the police?"

"Emilia, don't do this, don't do this, don't."

"So you knew everything, apart from who did it?"

"No. I don't know how it felt."

"Well, what do you want to know about him?"

"Was it somebody you knew?"

"No."

"What kind of person was it?"

"Not a particularly nice one."

Bruch slams his fist into the bed. He roars with frustration.

"We won't get any further if we don't do anything about this."

"What do you mean by further?" she says coldly. "Where is it you want to go?"

"Further! With you!"

"And we can't go on?"

"No, we can't go on like this."

"What does 'can't go on like this' mean?"

"That we can't go on like this any longer. Something has to happen."

"You knew all along."

"Emilia."

"The whole fucking time."

"Emilia."

"I tried so hard not to let it matter, to protect you and me and our love from it. And now it turns out that it was a lie from the start. Everything has always been soiled by it."

"Emilia."

"Stop saying my name all the time."

"Please." Bruch was crying. She needed to tell him they'd just made a child. She burst out laughing at the thought of it. She folded her arms across her stomach and crawled away under the covers. She started hiccoughing under there and after a few minutes she no longer knew whether she was laughing or crying. A child. And a marriage that can't go on any longer. What now? She thought of Vincent, who, behind every glance at her, even the last one, in his deplorable state, there on Spuistraat, had kept her secret. So that's what he'd meant when he said she could keep a secret. It was a good thing Bruch was scared of Jacob, otherwise he'd no doubt have gone and consulted him too, a psychiatrist, after all, someone who surely must have a bit of advice to share. Maybe Jacob was the only person who really knew her, who knew her without everything that over the years had attached itself to her like moss.

Pieces of agricultural plastic are bobbing about in the water. She recognizes the red of the kitchen, too, chunks of it floating into a corner. If she stretches out her foot she can touch the water. Cold. She feels its crude, remorseless power. The water won't make any distinction, won't have any motives. It'll drag off, as is its nature, whatever isn't firmly fixed down. Drowning won't be at all hard. She pulls up her knees and wraps her arms around them.

Bruch went on speaking to her but she pressed her hands to her ears and heard only the melody of his voice, strikingly rhythmical and strikingly monotone. Was the man talking in monosyllables perhaps? Or was he simply chopping all the syllables apart? After a while the alarm clock went off again. Bruch left the room, punctual as he was, relieved too, probably, to be able to get away from her and closer to more concrete problems. She thrust her hands between her legs. A child, she thought. Then she crept out from under the covers.

She picked up Bruch's book, by Dostoevsky, and read a few pages before suddenly remembering the content of the novel, which she'd once read, the rejection of the average person, the refusal to crawl under the bell-shaped safety of the average, the refusal to adopt any position other than that of the exception, despising the very safety she'd sought. She looked around the attic, searching for a way out, and gathered her clothes together, but she was trembling too much, her teeth were chattering, her shoulders had cramped up and her skull felt as if it might burst. The normal distribution wasn't the right model at all—an error typical of statisticians: relying on the wrong model. She'd have done better to apply the improper distribution, the improper prior that stretches endlessly in all directions, an open plain like the surface of water, without peaks, without hiding places. Then she wouldn't have been so deceived.

There was a noise from downstairs, the sound of splitting timber. Maybe the house was collapsing. If so, this house had impeccable timing. At last she managed to get her sweatpants and T-shirt on, and crawled back into bed where she gradually began to feel less cold and to relax. She dreamed she was bound to a wheel that was spinning faster and faster. The radio spewed out news reports, interrupted by loud syncopated music lacking in harmony. From time to time she caught a glimpse of Bruch standing in a corner of the room looking at her. She remembered fighting with him, remembered him trying to pull her upright, shouting, slapping her face. She had a clear image of his bloodied face above hers.

"We need to get out of here. Come on Emilia, darling, wake up. Can you stand?"

The sound of the helicopter is getting louder. A tinny amplified voice is calling out to her.

"Mrs. Roovers. Can you hear me? We're coming to help you. Emilia Roovers. Can you hear me? Try to open an upstairs window." She stands up and goes to the bedroom. She opens the window at the back. Ahead of her stretches a wild grey sea, with trees in it and other objects floating. The daylight pierces her head like shrapnel. A helicopter is hovering above what was once their garden; its side is open and a man is waving to her. He stretches his arms towards her. Wind, caused by the turning rotors, flings the curtain into her face. A police launch skims across the water and stops right under the window. In the boat are two men, both in uniform. They're beckoning to her. Is she being rescued?

Come on now, one of them gestures with his arms, his lips forming words she can't understand. *Come on now.* She thinks of what Blanche Dubois says at the end of the play, as she's led away by people in white coats. *I have always depended on the kindness of strangers.* She's put her sweatpants on back to front, she notices now. And she's got no shoes on her feet. She climbs onto the windowsill. The men are close by. One of them shouts something unintelligible. The helicopter is making a terrible racket. A man grabs her ankles and she carefully bends towards him. She wraps her arms around his neck, lays her cheek against the rough, stiff fabric of his jacket and slides down. He smells of diesel. She bangs her hip against something. He lowers her into the boat. Nothing can abolish the loneliness. There are only stopgaps, distractions. Branches have been laid over the pit, branches and grass to make you think you have ground under your feet when in fact it's an abyss. The helicopter sweeps round in a wide arc, gains height, and disappears eastwards.

"Good day, madam. I'm Harold, will you come this way?" He has a pleasant voice, at least. And ginger hair.

"Your husband's already with us."

"Oh really?"

He throws a blanket around her and packs her feet in a second blanket. The other man nods to her and says something into a walkie-talkie. The first man sits on a seat opposite her while the other one opens the throttle.

"We're taking you somewhere warm and dry. Everything's going to be fine."

After finishing her studies at the University of Manchester, **LIZ WATERS** worked for some years with English-language texts and at a literary agency in Amsterdam before becoming a full-time translator of literary fiction and non-fiction. Authors whose books she has translated include Lieve Joris, Jaap Scholten, Luuk van Middelaar, Annelies Verbeke, and Geert Mak.

Book Club Discussion Guides are available on our website

By the same author:
Love, If That's What It Is

World Editions promotes voices from around the globe by publishing books from many different countries and languages in English translation. Through our work, we aim to enhance dialogue between cultures, foster new connections, and open doors which may otherwise have remained closed.

Also available from World Editions:

The Leash and the Ball
Rodaan Al Galidi
Translated by Jonathan Reeder
"Al Galidi has an eye for the absurd."
—*Irish Times*

Cocoon
Zhang Yueran
Translated by Jeremy Tiang
"An incisive portrait of a generation."
—*Le Courrier Suisse*

Tale of the Dreamer's Son
Preeta Samarasan
"Samarasan's inventive prose is stunning."
—*The Guardian*

Abyss
Pilar Quintana
Translated by Lisa Dillman
"Small details that can define an entire continent."
—*Vogue*

The Gospel According to the New World
Maryse Condé
Translated by Richard Philcox
"Condé has a gift for storytelling."
—*New York Times Book Review*

On the Design

As book design is an integral part of the reading experience, we would like to acknowledge the work of those who shaped the form in which the story is housed.

Tessa van der Waals (Netherlands) is responsible for the cover design, cover typography, and art direction of all World Editions books. She works in the internationally renowned tradition of Dutch Design. Her bright and powerful visual aesthetic maintains a harmony between image and typography, and captures the unique atmosphere of each book. She works closely with internationally celebrated photographers, artists, and letter designers. Her work has frequently been awarded prizes for Best Dutch Book Design.

The shape and color of the typography of *Breakwater* on the cover represent an icebreaker, with the background blue reminiscent of water. The blue background is meant to have a hairy and tactile appearance, giving it an intensity that also suggests movement and touch. Water plays a major role in the book, rising water acting as a symbol for the eruption of hidden feelings. The title in the original Dutch is *Noodweer*, which means both "self-defense" and "storm." We tried to capture both these elements with the English title *Breakwater*, a structure that is itself a defense against the sea's force. The font used for the title is from TypeType foundry and is called TT Norms.

The cover has been edited by lithographer Bert van der Horst of BFC Graphics (Netherlands).

Euan Monaghan (United Kingdom) is responsible for the typography and careful interior book design.

The text on the inside covers and the press quotes are set in Circular, designed by Laurenz Brunner (Switzerland) and published by Swiss type foundry Lineto.

All World Editions books are set in the typeface Dolly, specifically designed for book typography. Dolly creates a warm page image perfect for an enjoyable reading experience. This typeface is designed by Underware, a European collective formed by Bas Jacobs (Netherlands), Akiem Helmling (Germany), and Sami Kortemäki (Finland). Underware are also the creators of the World Editions logo, which meets the design requirement that "a strong shape can always be drawn with a toe in the sand."